PU

Wyvern Spring

Toby Forward was born in Coventry. He went to college to pursue theological training and subsequently became a parish priest. He is now a full-time writer and lives with his wife and two daughters near Hull.

Other books by Toby Forward

THE TOAD LADY
TRAVELLING BACKWARDS
WYVERN AUTUMN
WYVERN SPRING
WYVERN SUMMER
WYVERN WINTER

Wyvern Spring

Toby Forward

Illustrated by
Michael Foreman

PUFFIN BOOKS

To Glen and Sue
Epithalamion 12th June 1993
with love

PUFFIN BOOKS

Published by the Penguin Group
Penguin Books Ltd, 27 Wrights Lane, London W8 5TZ, England
Penguin Books USA Inc., 375 Hudson Street, New York, New York 10014, USA
Penguin Books Australia Ltd, Ringwood, Victoria, Australia
Penguin Books Canada Ltd, 10 Alcorn Avenue, Toronto, Ontario, Canada M4V 3B2
Penguin Books (NZ) Ltd, 182–190 Wairau Road, Auckland 10, New Zealand

Penguin Books Ltd, Registered Offices: Harmondsworth, Middlesex, England

First published by Andersen Press Limited 1993
Published in Puffin Books 1994
1 3 5 7 9 10 8 6 4 2

Text copyright © Toby Forward, 1993
Illustrations copyright © Michael Foreman, 1993
All rights reserved

The moral right of the author and illustrator has been asserted

Printed in England by Clays Ltd, St Ives plc

Dust are our frames; and, gilded dust, our pride
Looks only for a moment whole and sound;
Like that long-buried body of the king,
Found lying with his urns and ornaments,
Which at a touch of light, an air of heaven,
Slipt into ashes, and was found no more.

Aylmer's Field
Tennyson

ONE

A car drew up outside the little old cottage.
Before the driver could turn the engine off there
was a crash and a yell. The driver looked
alarmed. The front door swung open and Thomas
ran out, his arms wide. Mrs Ketch, warm in the
back seat, smiled and wound down the window.
Thomas pulled at the door and nearly flung himself into the car.

'Careful,' laughed his mother.

7

'You're better,' he said.

'I'm back,' she said.

A tall figure appeared in the open doorway, holding what was left of a vase.

'It doesn't matter,' said Mrs Ketch.

'Sorry,' said Thomas. 'I'll get you another.'

'I never liked it anyway,' she said. Thomas jumped out and she followed him, carefully, taking her time to stand up and making sure she was steady by touching her fingers on the roof of the car.

'Hello,' said Thomas's father, as though to a stranger. The pieces of vase kept his hands busy.

'Hello,' she said. She smiled, leaned up and kissed him on the cheek.

The driver opened the boot of the car, took out a small suitcase and looked around him. The cottage stood on the edge of a village green, ragged and untidy with the muddy edges and coarse grass of early spring. In the middle of the green, with her back to the old Manor House and facing across the fields, stood a statue of a woman in old-fashioned clothes. 'Bit parky,' he said, as the wind poked cold fingers into his sleeves and neck.

'Come on in,' said Mrs Ketch. 'I'll make us all a warm drink.'

A tall figure, in black, stood watching them from the doorway of the church on the other side of the green. Thomas frowned. The figure raised a great arm and waved. Mrs Ketch lifted her arm in response, wincing a little.

'Does it still hurt?' asked Thomas. 'I thought they'd made it better.'

'They have,' she said. 'It is better. I'm just not used to being able to move it. I think it's going to hurt, so I do that. But then it doesn't.'

The driver told her how much the fare was.

'You'll have that drink?' she said.

He looked up at the front of the cottage. A long banner hung from the window and writhed and flapped in the wind, making a snapping noise as it doubled back on itself and then unwound again. WELLCOME HOME. The words, difficult to read as the banner swirled and streamed, came from the mouth of a green dragon, with leather wings and eagle's legs. The mouth was wide with, to the driver's mind, more menace than welcome. A hot cup of tea would be just the ticket – get him warm for the drive back to town. The huge man was bearing down on him, black cloak flapping, large feet tramping muddy craters. He reached the group, put out his hand and grasped the case. His cuff fell back and revealed a purple snake tattooed on his arm. The wind, whipping up more fiercely, flapped the dragon and made a howling noise from the chimneys of the empty Manor. The driver shuddered from something more penetrating than the edge of the wind. He glanced over his shoulder and saw that two dragons, carved in stone – he hoped – were perched on the gateposts of the great house. 'No,' he decided. 'No time for a drink. Got to get back. Lots to do.'

The big man sensed the driver's unease and he threw back his head and laughed, a deep, mocking laugh.

The driver pocketed the fare, threw the car into gear and screeched away.

'Welcome home,' said the priest. 'Though that's not how you spell it, Thomas.'

'Thank you, Mr Weever,' said Mrs Ketch. 'It's good to be back.'

'It's the old-fashioned spelling,' lied Thomas.

'Cup of tea, Vicar?' said Mr Ketch.

'You'll want to be on your own for a while,' said Weever. 'I'll call another day.' He handed the case to Thomas. 'Good wyvern, though,' he complimented him, indicating the dragon banner.

'He's all wyverns these days,' said Mr Ketch.

'He's a Ketch,' said Weever.

Thomas's father nodded. 'And you're a Weever,' he said.

The vicar and Mr Ketch looked steadily at each other for a while. 'You know that much?' said Weever at last.

'It's in the old songs,' said Mr Ketch.

'Does Thomas know them?'

'Some. Not the Weever songs.'

10

'Come on, Mum, you'll get cold.' Thomas tugged at her coat and led her into the cottage. He closed the door behind them.

Ted Ketch and Weever stood a long time talking in the wind.

The fire lit the room in the late afternoon dusk, throwing orange patterns on the old walls. Thomas took his mother's coat, hung it up and put another log on the fire.

'I'll make tea,' she said.

'Sit down,' said Thomas. 'I've got it all ready.'

'I'm a lot better,' she smiled.

'Just a minute.'

Mrs Ketch sat in her own chair, kicked off her shoes and warmed her toes. She stretched, happily, then felt a small stab of pain in her shoulder and stopped. Clinks and rattles drifted through the kitchen door.

'Don't break anything else,' she warned Thomas.

'Ready in a minute,' he called back.

She glanced through the window and was surprised to see that her husband was as tall as Weever, and nearly as broad. Ted Ketch was such a gentle man, so private and quiet that she hardly noticed any more how big he was. It was different with the new vicar, loud and headstrong and so direct.

Thomas kicked open the door and carried in a tray. Tea cups, milk jug, tea pot, and a plate of biscuits.

'I made them,' he said.

He poured the tea carefully.

'Oh, they're lovely,' she said. And she leaned forward and kissed him. It was the first kiss since she had returned.

'They're cinnamon,' he said. 'And I dusted the heads with ginger, to make them hot.'

The biscuits were shaped like wyverns, the two-legged dragons on the gateposts of the Manor and on his welcome home banner.

'And the eyes,' said his mother. 'So fierce. So orange.'

'Candied peel,' he said. 'It took me ages to think of something orange you could eat.'

'But how clever,' she praised him.

'Miss Aylmer told me,' he said, dropping his head.

'But you cut them and baked them.'

'Yes,' he cheered up.

Mrs Ketch rummaged around in her handbag. She produced a small stone wyvern and placed it on the tray next to the biscuits. 'They're perfect,' she said. 'But why have you made the eyes orange? They aren't on the ones on the Manor.'

'Real ones are,' he said.

There was a silence while they sipped their tea. Outside, the deep voice of the vicar rumbled on.

'How did you make them fly?' she asked

12

at last.

'I don't know.'

'Can you do it again?'

'I don't know.'

Thomas picked up a biscuit and bit off the head of the wyvern. His mother looked anxious.

'It's not a game,' she said.

Thomas nodded.

'You can't make a pet out of a wyvern.'

Thomas picked up the small stone figure. 'It made you better, didn't it?'

'Who knows,' said his mother. 'Perhaps it was the doctors.'

Thomas squeezed the wyvern. 'It was broken off the Kych Stone, in the church,' he said. 'You know that.' He closed his eyes and recited,

'Reach out and touch this carved stone
If you are sick and would be whole.
For Thomas Kych of Herpeton
Has caused this tablet to be put
Where all may use its potency.
These birds and beasts that here are shewn
And snakes, and creatures of the pond
Will all conjoin at his command
To heal all manner of disease
That he has power to put away
Through his familiarity
With wyverns and with creatures all.
And if this remedy should fail,

13

Then seek out Master Kych, his book
And he will give you remedy.'

His green eyes shone in the firelight. 'It made you better,' he insisted.

'I'm back,' she said. 'And I'm very pleased to be here.'

The door swung open. Weever's head poked through. 'Thomas,' he said. 'Do you want to come across to Miss Aylmer's with me?'

Thomas squeezed his mother's hand.

'Go on,' she said. 'I'm back, now. Plenty of time.'

Thomas darted out.

Mr Ketch dropped the pieces of vase into the fire grate and poured more tea, using Thomas's cup for himself. He put a large hand on his wife's small one. 'I'm glad you're back,' he said, shyly.

She rested against him. 'I've missed it,' she said. 'You. Thomas. This place.'

The last of the light outside had drained away and they sat in the orange of the fire.

'I'm sorry about the vase,' he said.

'It doesn't matter.'

'It was your favourite.'

'Never mind. It was old.'

Ted Ketch sighed. 'It was your grandmother's.'

'And not new when she got it.'

'The old things,' said Ted. 'They're coming back.'

14

'That vase isn't,' she laughed.

He looked troubled. 'There'll be trouble.'

'Will Thomas be all right? Should we let him do all this with the wyverns?'

'We've got no choice. He's a Ketch.'

'So are you.'

'But it ignored me. It's his turn.'

'And Weever. Is he all right?'

Ted snapped the wings off a wyvern biscuit. 'You can never tell. Not with Weevers.'

Across the green, Thomas and the big man opened the door of Viviper Cottage.

'He says they've found a book,' said Ted.

'Thomas Kych's book?'

'A book.'

'Will he be all right?'

TWO

Viviper Cottage was hotter even than Thomas's.

'I have to keep it warm for the snakes,' Miss Aylmer had told Thomas.

Sometimes Miss Aylmer had the glass tanks of snakes all over the place, but usually they were tucked away out of sight where they could not frighten the few visitors who called. Miss Aylmer was new to the village, and Herpeton had not taken to her. Her harsh, American voice, her severe bun of grey hair, but most of all her direct way of asking questions and giving her frank opinion had not won her many friends.

'It's a bit early for frogspawn,' said Thomas, peering into the murky water.

'Not if you know where to look,' she said. 'The streams are no good. The water runs too fast and makes it too cold. But there are places at the edge of the Stone Pond, where the trees overhang. It's where you'll always find the first frogspawn.'

'Shouldn't you leave it there?'

'Might freeze over. I'll take care.'

'Why is it called Stone Pond?' asked Weever. 'It's a long way from Parcel's Stones.'

'It's always been called that,' said Thomas.

'That's no answer.'

'Your mother's better?' asked Miss Aylmer.

'Thank you, yes,' said Thomas.

'The Kych Stone cured her,' said Weever.

Miss Aylmer shrugged. 'It won't have done her any harm,' she grated. 'Is she properly better? For good?'

'Yes,' said Thomas, quickly.

'So you won't want to look for the book?' asked Weever.

Thomas bit his lip. 'Well,' he said. 'We don't need it to make Mum better, but it might, er, it might help other people,' he said.

Miss Aylmer laughed.

Thomas scowled.

Weever nodded. 'And it might help you to learn how to make the wyverns fly,' he said.

'All right,' said Thomas. 'It might. And it will keep Parcel away,' he added, pleased to have found another reason.

'He's gone, now,' said Weever.

'Wait and see,' warned Miss Aylmer. 'Wait and see.'

'He knows,' said Thomas. 'He can't come back. We know about him now.'

A door creaked and a slim form slid across the floor. It made the middle of the room, reared up and spread its hood out, swaying its head from side to side and looking first at Weever, then at Thomas.

'Careful,' said Miss Aylmer. 'I don't milk him any more. One bite and you're dead.'

The cobra turned as she spoke, then looked away, forked tongue flickering in and out.

Weever put his hand out, exposing the snake tattoo on his left wrist. The snake slid away from him and moved to Thomas.

'Hello, Shakti,' whispered Thomas. 'Come on, then,' as the snake slid up to him. He hummed a wordless tune and Shakti settled on his lap.

'Can I see the book?' he asked.

'You've waited a long time to ask.' Weever looked directly at Thomas. 'You don't trust me.'

'I wanted Mum back from hospital first,' said Thomas. 'Before I looked at the book.'

'Before you could ask?'

'I didn't want to see it, in case it stopped her getting better.'

'It isn't Thomas Kych's book,' Weever warned him.

'I know that. But it did belong to him?'

'Yes.'

'And you stole it?'

'I found it in a box in the County Archives. It belongs to the church. I'm the vicar. I've got every right to look after it.'

Thomas took the book from Miss Aylmer. He sniffed the leather of the binding, like a dog. He turned it over in his hands, smiling at the thick paper, the dark cover, the indented figure of a wyvern, once gilt, now almost brown save for a few grains of gold.

'I'm afraid you can't take it away,' said Miss Aylmer.

'He did,' said Thomas.

Weever glared.

'He's only the vicar. I'm Thomas Ketch. This is my book.'

'You didn't know there was any such thing until I told you,' said Weever.

'As what?' Thomas challenged him. 'As the book?'

'As Thomas Ketch,' Weever exploded. 'You didn't think your name meant any more than your friend Jack Roberts's.'

'Or Weever?' said Thomas. 'What about

Weever? What does that mean?'

Weever slumped back in his chair, his weight making it creak with discomfort. 'More than you think, maybe,' he said.

'This won't get us anywhere,' said Miss Aylmer. 'Are we working together, or not?'

'Ask him,' said Thomas.

'Well?' she asked Weever.

He glared at her.

'You can take the book away, Thomas,' she said. 'You're right. It's more yours than anyone else's.'

Weever sat up in the chair and gripped the arms. Shakti drew back, ready to strike.

Thomas smiled. 'I'll leave it here,' he agreed. 'It's safer.'

Weever relaxed.

'But don't let *him* take it away,' said Thomas. 'I want it to stay here.'

'That's a deal,' she agreed.

Thomas turned the book round in his hands.

'How old is it?' he asked.

'No one knows. There's no date on the Kych Stone. No records of Thomas Kych.' Miss Aylmer peered over Thomas's shoulder.

'Sit at the table,' suggested Weever. 'We can all look at it together.'

'You've seen it already,' said Thomas.

'That's not the point,' he said. 'I want to see what you look at.'

20

'What's in it?'

'Lots of things. Old recipes, lists of names, places, poems. He drew a lot, as well. But none of it is any help. And it isn't *the* book,' Weever explained. 'I've spent hours and hours on it, and it's no help at all.'

Thomas opened the book while the two others looked over.

'It's not English,' he said, with disappointment.

'Of a sort,' said Miss Aylmer. 'And his writing's not easy. Try.'

'It's neat writing,' said Thomas. 'But I can't make it out.'

'But he forms his letters in an old way,' Weever said with impatience. 'Look.'

Thomas was turning the pages with a regular movement, not stopping to try to read.

'The pictures are good,' he said.

'Perhaps you'd like to colour them in,' said Weever.

Thomas snapped the book shut.

'Careful!'

'Clovis, would you like to go and pour yourself a drink?' suggested Miss Aylmer.

Weever stood up meaningfully and walked away.

'This page, I think,' said Miss Aylmer, finding where Thomas had reached.

Thomas leaned over. 'Look,' he said. Many of the pages were covered in Thomas Kych's neat hand, all over with no margin, but some were illustrated in the text, some were whole pages of intricate drawings, some, like this double page, had the writing set in the middle of a border of ink lines. 'What's this?' asked Thomas.

'It's the Kych Stone,' said Miss Aylmer. The Kych Stone was a tablet in the wall of the church. In the centre was the verse Thomas had recited to his mother, and around the edge was a carved frame, with plants and flowers and all sorts of animals.

Weever swigged hard at a glass of whisky. 'Just a copy,' he said. 'I've looked at it already.'

'No,' said Thomas. 'There are fifteen lines in the Kych Stone. Only thirteen here. See.'

Weever came back and stood over Thomas. He screwed up his eyes and read, with difficulty,

> 'Thomas Kych of Herpeton
> Has hidden his secret in his
> Book where none may read —
> It will be well concealed – Be
> Guarded by this advice – Beware
> The wyvern – A man
> Who would find this secret and use
> It must first take heed and
> Delve deep below the wyvern stone far from
> Stone Pond – in Parcel's Stones —
> Take the key from the timbers of
> The buried ship – Nor wake the sleeping
> King.'

Miss Aylmer sighed with pleasure. 'See,' she said. 'It's not the same as the Kych Stone. It's something new. Something important. And he found it. Straight away. You'd looked indeed!' She snorted.

Weever filled his glass again. 'It's hard work,' he said, 'reading that writing. I wasn't going to bother with something I'd already seen.'

'But you hadn't,' said Thomas in triumph. 'You hadn't seen it.'

Miss Aylmer laid her hand on his arm and silenced him.

Weever took another angry swig, glowered at Thomas, then threw back his head and roared with laughter. 'All right, Thomas Ketch,' he said. 'You win.' He ruffled the auburn hair, something Thomas hated, but he knew it was a way of making up again. 'Look,' he went on. 'You're Thomas Ketch, and you don't have to prove anything. All right?'

'And you don't have to keep on needling him,' said Miss Aylmer. 'All right?' She took Weever's glass from him, drank deeply and returned it. 'Pour us a couple more, will you? And something for Thomas.'

Thomas was bent over the book. 'What's this?' he asked. 'Blaceberian? Is it a person, or a place?'

Weever looked, putting his thick finger on the book. 'Sounds like a place to me,' he said. 'Nowhere I know.' He moved his lips as he read the rest of the words on that page. 'Pott?' he murmured. 'What's that?'

'It's a pot,' said Miss Aylmer. 'And that's a recipe for blackberry jam you're looking at.'

'Oh, yes,' said Weever. 'That's right.'

'Can't you read it?' asked Thomas.

'It's all right once you know what it's about,' explained Miss Aylmer. 'Then the words make sense.'

'Is there lots of rubbish like that?'

'Rubbish?' She arched her eyebrows.

'Jam recipes.'

'It's a very good recipe.'

Thomas gave her a hard look. 'You haven't had this book long enough to know,' he said. 'You got it at Christmas. It's April now. No black-berries.'

Weever laughed.

Miss Aylmer smiled.

Shakti slid on to the table and over the book.

'It's a very common recipe,' she said, looking down at the page. 'I've used it lots of times.'

Thomas opened the book at another page at random. 'Here's something about wyverns,' he said. The excitement in his voice made Weever jump. 'Look. Wefan. That must be wyvern,' said Thomas, proud that he was getting used to trans-lating the old words.

Miss Aylmer shook her head. 'No,' she said. 'That isn't wyvern. Try somewhere else.'

24

Weever leaned on the table, his hands clenched against the wood. The cuffs of his cassock drawn back as he stretched forward.

Thomas ran his finger over the page. 'Here it is again,' he said. 'Wefer. And here's a picture of one.'

Beneath the word WEFER was a drawing of a man, arms upraised, long cloak swept back by the wind, a mane of wild black hair. Above him, as though summoned, flew a wyvern, mouth wide, wings outstretched. Beneath the man, in purple ink, almost black with age, writhed a snake.

'See,' Thomas insisted. 'Wefer – wyvern. And there it is.'

'That's not the wyvern,' said Miss Aylmer, quietly. 'That's the man. Wefer – Weever.'

Thomas looked aside at the bare forearm of the priest, the purple snake tattoo disappearing up the cuff of the black cassock.

Weever threw back his huge head and laughed, his wild hair streaming out like a lion's mane.

THREE

Stone Pond stood outside the village of Herpeton. From its rim a sharp eye could just catch a glimpse of the very tops of the tall grey monoliths which made the ancient circle of Parcel's Stones. In another direction the spire of the church on its high mound pierced the sky, or rather, the spire itself was hidden but the dull, bronze weather vane – a wyvern, wings outstretched, rode the clouds. Thomas poked a black stick into the muddy edge of the pond. He drew it out and it made a low, squelching noise.

Jack laughed. 'Was that you?' he shouted across the pond.

Clare, Jack's sister, threw a stick across at him. It dropped short, but landed near enough to him to splash him with the cold, brown water. Jack found a stone and flung it over, letting it arc high and drop, but the pond was quite large, about as wide across as Wivern Manor on the village green, and his shot fell short, dropping harmlessly into the water with a plop.

Thomas stood to attention and listened.

The three children were at different points around the pond – at twelve, four and eight o'clock. Towser, Jack's dog, was at no fixed point, but then he never was. His legs drove him round and round the pond, sometimes slipping and sending him into the reedy shallows, where his short, spaniel's legs were hopelessly beaten even by the low edge and his stomach became soaked with water and caked with mud.

'What was that?' he asked.

'What?' said Clare.

'I thought I heard something.' He stared hard into the pond, where Jack's stone had landed.

'A dragon,' said Jack. 'He's heard a dragon!' And he snarled.

'Oh, shut up!' said Clare.

Thomas looked intently at the water.

'A clunk,' he said. 'Like two stones knocking together.'

Jack, meanwhile, was flapping his arms and leaping in the air. 'Thomas Ketch – the Dragonmaster,' he yelled. 'I can fly.'

Thomas realised that something was going on at the other side of the pond and he looked over.

Jack snarled again.

Thomas blushed, making his pale face red and his freckles almost disappear.

'Shut up,' repeated Clare. 'It's stupid.'

Jack began to feel a little foolish under Thomas's stare and he dropped his arms to his side and stopped growling. 'Not as stupid as him,' he said. 'The Dragonmaster.'

This was a row that had been nearly three months coming and Thomas knew he could not turn aside from it.

'Go on, Jack,' he said. He wished he could say it quietly, but he had to shout it across the still water of the pond.

'Nothing,' said Jack. 'Forget it.'

This was what Jack had been saying since Christmas.

'No. Go on.'

Jack tossed another, smaller stone into the pond. 'Hear anything?' he asked. A small frond of steam came from his mouth, warm air against the spring cold. 'You're always going on about it,' he said. 'Dragons.'

'Wyverns!' shouted Clare. 'They're wyverns.'

'Same thing,' said Jack. His straight black hair framed his face. A casual observer would have found it difficult to know him from his sister.

'I only said I heard a noise,' said Thomas.

'That's how it always starts,' said Jack. 'You say something like that, and then, the next thing, you're talking dragons and –'

'Wyverns!' shouted Clare.

Jack ignored her. ' – and how you can make them fly over the village. Well, it's stupid and I'm fed up with it. It's a kids' game.'

'You were there,' said Thomas. 'When they flew. You saw them.'

'It was a trick of the light,' said Jack. 'There's no such thing.'

'Why did Parcel run away?' asked Clare. 'You're so clever. Why did he run away?'

'Weever came, didn't he?' shouted Jack. 'And old Aylmer. They frightened him off.'

Thomas thrust his hands in his pockets and looked at Jack.

'I'm fed up with it,' said Jack. He flung another stone, hard, fast and low. It skimmed the water, turned in the air and splashed right in front of Thomas, soaking his trousers. Towser snarled, quivered and set off at a terrific pace, round the pond and flung himself at Jack, snarling. Jack's jaw dropped and he pushed Towser away. The dog crouched, bared his teeth and menaced Jack.

'My own dog!' Jack shouted. 'Look! You've even taken my own dog away from me.'

He turned and ran off, kicking mud behind him in his speed.

Thomas stood and watched him go. Clare walked round the pond and joined Thomas.

'He'll be all right,' she said. 'He'll come round.'

'I don't think so,' said Thomas.

'He was there,' she said. 'He saw the wyverns. He knows they flew.'

'That's what I don't understand,' said Thomas.

'What?'

'There were the three of us, and Weever and Miss Aylmer, and Harry Dodds, and my dad. We all saw them fly. Real dragons, in the sky.'

'And Parcel,' added Clare.

'He doesn't count,' said Thomas. 'He's the enemy.'

'So what? He saw them.'

'But he wouldn't tell,' said Thomas. 'But with all of us, why isn't it in the newspapers, or on the telly, or something?'

'I'd never thought of that,' said Clare.

'Why doesn't the whole village know about it? There must have been people looking out of their windows. They must have seen.'

'In the middle of the night?'

'There's always someone can't sleep.'

They poked around in the water silently for a while.

'I don't know what we're doing,' said Clare at last.

No answer from Thomas.

'There's a bit of frogspawn,' said Clare. 'I thought we were looking for that.'

'We are,' said Thomas. He produced a jar from the pocket of his duffel coat and scooped some of the black-speckled jelly into it.

'No we aren't,' said Clare. 'You could have done that half an hour ago.'

'I'll tell you what I think it is,' said Thomas.

'What?' asked Clare, eagerly.

'Some of them – Parcel, Weever, maybe even Harry Dodds – don't want to talk about the wyverns, because they know something.'

'Yes.'

'And the others, like Jack, won't believe it.'

'But he saw it.'

'Makes no difference,' said Thomas. 'Just won't believe it. You heard him just then.'

'But why?'

'Don't know.'

Thomas held the jar up to look in it.

'You pig,' said Clare.

'Eh?'

'You're saying this so you don't have to tell me what we're looking for here. What is it?'

Thomas grinned. 'All right,' he said. 'But it's cold. Let's go inside.'

Jack came to a halt at the edge of the circle of great grey pillars which was Parcel's Stones. He leaned against one, feeling very daring. For as long as they could remember, the children had avoided the circle. When he came to think about it, no one went there, not even grown-ups. It was haunted. No, they had grown too old for that game. Then it was dangerous, marshy in the middle, you would be sucked down into the earth. But they had never put that idea to the test. Or it was just dangerous to be away from the houses that far. Anyone might see you and there were some terrible people about. A policewoman and a policeman had come to school and given them a talk about not going to lonely places. But that wasn't the reason. After all, Stone Pond and the Barrow were no less lonely than the stones, yet they played there. This was the first time Jack had ever touched one of the rough-hewn giants.

When he had got his breath back, Jack rubbed his hands against the surface. It was smooth, yet jagged and uneven, hacked out from some quarry bed how many years ago?

He liked the texture beneath his hands.

Cautiously he moved round the stone, keeping his back to it, until he stood inside the circle, looking round.

Jack had heard people talk about their hair standing on end, but he had never felt it. Even when he had been locked in the Manor and all the snakes had slithered in, even then, though he had been terrified, he had not felt his scalp prick. But now he had to put his hand to his head to make sure that his hair was not on end.

It was like the feeling you got when you made electricity with a comb and let it lift your hair. No, it was more like the feeling on your arms, when the goose flesh raised small bumps.

Jack waited, watching. Nothing happened. He stepped forward, one small pace. The ground was firm beneath his foot.

The wind whipped round the stones, making a low, moaning noise, but Jack was not to be put off by that. He knew the wind, even if he did not know a ghost.

He stepped further in.

Measuring the distance with his eye, he guessed the circle was about the same distance across as Stone Pond. There were a lot of broken stones, all sizes, lying about in the circle. Jack picked up a small rock and tossed it, to see. It fell just inside the circle at the other side. Jack nodded. About the same. He moved further in.

At every step it became easier to go on. The tension left him and he grew confident.

He was not quite halfway across.

Turning slowly, he tried to count the stones. He picked a big one and counted from there. Then he tried it again in the other direction. It was difficult, because some of the stones seemed to be missing. There were gaps he'd never noticed before, from outside. Again. Different total. Again. Different again. Once more. The first number returned. That must be it. Once more to make sure. No. Different again. He gave up. It was making him feel dizzy.

Perhaps if he stood right in the centre?

But that was an old problem. How do you find the exact centre of a big space, without a piece of string or something?

Easy. Jack gasped. Too easy by far. He found himself staring down at a circular slab set in what he was sure must be the dead centre of the Parcel's Stones. It was smooth, and so flat to the earth that it was invisible until you were right up to it. He reached down to touch it, and this time he was sure that the hair really did stand right out from his head. It was as sudden as an electric shock. Jack's fingers confirmed what his eyes had told him. Carved in the flat stone was a wyvern, flying free.

'You can do that,' said a harsh voice.

Jack spun round. 'What?'

'You can make the wyverns fly.'

Jack kept his fingers on the flat stone.

'That's nothing. Just a stone slab. There's wyverns all over Herpeton.'

'How can I make them fly?' asked Jack.

'Well, it's like this. Thomas Ketch, he can do it because he's a Ketch. But the rest of us, we

34

need the book. Thomas Kych's book.' A hand reached down and clasped Jack's. Above the hand, a snake, tattooed on the forearm. 'And whoever can make the wyverns fly can do other things.'

'What?'

'Find treasure. Would you like to find treasure?'

Jack nodded.

'Make people better if they're ill. Make them ill if you want to hurt them.'

'I wouldn't want to do that.'

'Oh, no?'

'Not make people ill.'

'No, we wouldn't do that. But you'll help me?'

Jack hesitated.

'I've helped you.'

'How?'

'I let you into the circle. No one comes into the circle unless I let them.'

Jack looked disbelieving.

'I've been watching you. You and young Thomas Ketch. He'll find the book soon enough, if I don't get there first.'

'Yes.'

'And he'll never let you use it to make the wyverns fly, will he?'

Jack shook his head.

'But, when he gets close, you stop him. Bring me the book, and I'll show you how to use

35

it. Right?'

Jack wrenched his hand free of the strong grip and sprinted out of the circle and away. He didn't look back.

Mrs Roberts set a plate of biscuits in front of Thomas and Clare. 'Eat them all, if you like,' she said.

Thomas took one and bit it. Clare crammed a whole one into her mouth and broke another in two, waiting for there to be space for it. Thomas dropped one secretly to the floor, for Towser.

'On second thoughts,' said her mother. She brought another plate and divided the biscuits. 'Now you can both take your time,' she said. 'I'll be out the back, firing the kiln.'

They waited until she had shut the back door.

'I thought she'd never go,' said Clare. 'Come on. Show me.'

Thomas took the piece of paper from a small wallet. He unfolded it and smoothed it out on the table.

'These are just a few,' he said. 'They told me to pick anything, just as it caught my fancy. There are hundreds more pictures.'

'What's this for?' Clare pointed to a five-pointed star.

'That had words on each point,' said Thomas. 'But I couldn't work them out. I only copied it because it's easy. See.' He picked up a pencil and drew another star on a piece of scrap paper, in one movement without lifting his hand from the sheet.

Thomas showed her a sort of seagull with a stick man beneath it. He explained that it was a wyvern and a man in a cloak.

'These are just to remind me,' he said. 'They're really good in the book.'

Clare kicked her chair away from the table. 'It's not very good,' she said. 'I'd rather see the proper book.'

'I don't think they'd let you see it,' he said.

Clare was cross. 'But it's your book, isn't it? It's not theirs.'

'Sort of.'

'You still haven't told me what we were doing at the pond.'

The back door clicked. Thomas put his finger to his lips.

They waited. Silence.

Clare looked out of the window. 'She's still firing,' she said. 'It takes ages. We're all right. Just the wind.'

Towser growled.

'All right,' said Clare, giving him a friendly prod with her toe. 'Shush.'

Thomas flicked the edge of the paper. 'You won't laugh?' he said.

'No.'

Thomas paused.

'I believe you,' said Clare. 'I saw the wyverns fly. I know it's true.'

'Weever laughed,' said Thomas. 'And he knows all about it. But he laughed.'

'I won't,' promised Clare.

Thomas unfolded another piece of paper.

'Wow,' said Clare. 'That's beautiful. Did you do that?'

'Miss Aylmer,' said Thomas. 'And she was so quick.'

'Is it from the book?'

'Yes.'

A wyvern, wings outspread, mouth ready to attack, guarded a nest. In the nest were five eggs, one of them broken quite in two, another with a crack, the other three intact. A tiny wyvern, perfectly formed, sprang from the broken shell.

'The wyverns haven't flown for hundreds of years,' said Thomas. 'I woke them at Christmas. They're abroad again. We don't know how many. We don't know when. But, if they're abroad, then they'll be laying eggs. We can find them.'

'At Stone Pond?'

'Perhaps.'

'Let's look again.' Clare leaped to her feet. Towser yelped and rushed round.

'Not yet,' said Thomas. 'Listen.' He pointed to the stick man. 'We think – Weever and Miss Aylmer think, that I can make the wyverns fly because I'm a Ketch, if only I can find out how.

But,' he tapped the paper with the crude drawing, 'there's another way. If you can get hold of the proper book, Thomas Kych's book, it tells you a way that other people, maybe anyone, can make them fly. And have power over them. That's what's happening here.'

'That's what Parcel wanted,' said Clare.

'Yes.'

'But he's gone,' she said. 'You sent the wyverns after him.'

'The thing is,' said Thomas, 'that – '

The back door slammed.

Clare rushed to the window. 'She's still out there.'

Jack pushed the kitchen door open.

Towser growled.

Thomas folded the papers quickly and pushed them into his pockets. 'I'll go,' he said to Clare.

Jack put his hand out. 'I'm sorry,' he said. 'Friends?'

Thomas nodded. 'All right.'

'Great,' said Clare.

'What are you doing?' said Jack.

Towser growled again.

FOUR

'The thing I don't understand, Felicity,' said Weever, 'is the way he found the answer and paid no attention to it at all.'

Miss Aylmer shook her head. 'It is strange,' she agreed. 'Unless . . .'

'Unless what?'

'Unless it isn't the answer at all.'

Weever snorted. 'Of course it's the answer,' he said. 'You only have to read it.' He flicked a piece of paper to her, on which he had written out the page from the book, in modern English.

'Thomas Kych of Herpeton
Has hidden his secret in his
Book where none may read —
It will be well concealed – Be
Guarded by this advice – Beware
The wyvern – A man
Who would find this secret and use
It must first take heed and
Delve deep below the wyvern stone far from
Stone Pond – in Parcel's Stones —
Take the key from the timbers of
The buried ship – Nor wake the sleeping
King.'

'So what do you think it means?' she asked.

Weever clicked his tongue. 'It means,' he said, 'that you go into Parcel's Stones, dig deep, and you'll find a king, buried in a long ship, the way they used to bury kings, and that the book, Thomas Kych's book, will be in the ship with him. It's obvious.'

'Too obvious, maybe,' she said. 'It doesn't say a book. It says a key.'

'Same thing,' said Weever. 'You often get that sort of thing.'

She raised her eyebrows.

'Some books are even called keys,' he pressed on. 'And on old maps the guide to the symbols is called a key. You see it all the time. I tell you, it's the book. It's his book.' He strode up and down the small room swishing his cassock against the chairs.

'Sit down, Clovis. You'll break something.'

He dropped into an armchair.

'I'm not convinced,' she said. 'Why didn't he bother with it?'

'He saw the other pictures.' Weever gave his roar of laughter. 'Dragon's eggs. Oh, dear.'

Felicity pursed her lips. 'We'll have to see about that.'

Weever chuckled. 'I expect he's gone looking for them.'

'Will he look for them?' she said.

Weever wiped his eyes. 'Oh, dear,' he said again. 'It was some sort of recipe, I bet. For wine. That biteth like a serpent. Did you read it?'

'I couldn't. It was in some sort of code.'

'Pah!' he snorted. 'Code. Old Kych was so drunk when he wrote out the recipe that he couldn't make his hand work properly.' He looked at an empty glass. 'Still,' he reflected, 'I wouldn't mind knowing the secret.'

'You know where the bottle is,' she said.

Weever filled his own glass and hers. 'The thing is,' he said. 'Be sensible. The page says "the secret in his Book". Then it tells you where to look. Then it says "Take the key". So it must be the same thing. Otherwise, he'd tell you what

42

the key fitted. Key's no good without a lock.' He drank deeply, hugged himself and put the glass down. 'We're there, Felicity,' he said. 'We're really there. He's led us straight to it.'

Felicity sipped her whisky.

'You don't mind if I ask just one or two questions?'

Weever looked truculent.

'First, there's the question of going into Parcel's Stones. Can you go in?'

'Well,' he admitted, 'I never have. No one has, unless they're working for Parcel. You know that.'

Felicity sipped her drink.

'What's inside the circle, I wonder?'

'Nothing. You can see that.'

'So, why does no one go in?'

'I tried it once. I felt sick, dizzy, as I got close. There's a sort of force that keeps you out. But it's only a feeling, not a barrier.'

'No one's ever got in, though, except they worked for Parcel. Remember those archaeologists who excavated the Barrow? They were going to investigate the circle, but they packed their bags and left.'

Weever laughed. 'Something frightened them in there. But we'll manage it. It's only a matter of getting up enough nerve.'

'We'll see,' she said.

He sniffed. 'Go on.'

43

'Second, where do we dig? It's a big circle.'

'In the middle,' he said, triumphantly. 'It's obvious.'

'Maybe too obvious.'

'Huh.'

'Third, we know that they buried kings in mounds, like the Barrow, not in the middle of stone circles, so why do you think we'll find a king, even if we can get in, even if we dig in the right place?'

Weever crashed his hand down on the table and his empty glass jumped. 'Because it says so in the book. And it's all we can do.'

Miss Aylmer nodded. 'Well,' she said. 'You've got something there.' She tugged at a strand of hair. 'There's something worrying me, though.'

'What's that?'

'He's hiding something. I know he is.'

'You're imagining it.'

'No. It's in the book. He was looking at things but not telling us. We need to know what he's interested in. We'll have to keep an eye on him. Find out.'

Weever growled. 'We'll follow the clues we've got,' he said. 'Dig in Parcel's Stones.'

'But we'll have to find a way of going into the circle, without attracting attention. Otherwise, Parcel will be on to us.'

'He's gone,' said Weever. 'We've seen him off.'

'So, what do we do?'

Weever tapped his finger against his cheek, thoughtfully.

'Will you dig?' she asked.

'Yes.'

'At night?'

'Hardly.'

'Then there'll be half the village watching you.'

'Mmm.'

'And the newspapers.'

'Newspapers?'

'Disturbing an ancient monument.'

'That's it!' He leaped to his feet. The chair groaned. 'We'll organise a proper dig. Invite the newspapers.'

Miss Aylmer considered. 'It might work. But why?'

Weever poured himself another drink. 'I'll find a map, in the church. Say it tells you where the burial chamber is.'

'You can't just find an old map.'

'I'll make one.'

'Pshaw.'

'No. You're right. I'll find one, but it will crumble to dust when it gets in the air. But I'll remember it.'

Weever grabbed the door handle.

'Where are you off to?'

'Got to go down to the crypt,' he said. 'I've been hearing noises down there. Must have a look.'

He stood in the open doorway. Miss Aylmer looked round him at the green.

Weever was chuckling. 'Those old coffins, down the crypt,' he said. 'They're falling to pieces. Anything could drop out of them. And a map, well you'd – '

Miss Aylmer had put her finger to her lips, but in his excitement Weever had ignored it. She kicked his leg.

'Ow! What?'

Felicity nodded towards the green. A man stood in the shadow of the statue of the woman. He looked straight at Weever and Miss Aylmer. He made no attempt to conceal the fact that he was listening to them.

Weever scowled.

The man smiled.

Weever strode over to him, the ground wet and soft beneath him. They met beneath the stone figure of the woman.

'Will you look at that?' said the man. He pointed to the writing on the plinth.

JANE GWYER
Born 1743
*who for twelve years was Mistress
of Wivern Manor, until her sudden
Disappearance in 1781. Mild of Manner,
yet she was Strong of Purpose, her
Desire always to Right wrongs. She*

was Even-handed to Creatures of
Whatsoever Estate, Conscientious in
her Duty, Faithful and Obedient as a
Daughter, Condescending to the Poor,
unmoved by the Pretentions of
the Great.
All Creatures of the Hearth and
Beasts of the Wild were her
Friends and knew no Fear where
she was, or where
She Is Now.

Underneath this message was carved the image of a winged dragon, with feet like an eagle and with a barbed serpent's tail.

'I don't know how you've got the nerve to come round here,' said Weever angrily.

'I live here,' said the man. 'That's my house.' He pointed to the Manor. 'Her house,' and he looked up at Jane Gwyer. 'Wherever she is now.'

'You clear out, Parcel,' said Weever. 'You're not wanted here. You'll be in trouble if you stay.'

Parcel nodded, calmly. 'I'll stay,' he said. 'And it's not me that'll be in trouble. Just you see.' He took a key from his pocket. 'I'll be off home, then,' he said.

'That's not your home,' said Weever. 'It never can be.'

'I bought it fair and square,' said Parcel. 'It's mine. Unless she wants to come back and get it,'

47

he added, looking at Jane Gwyer again. He gave a short laugh, more like a bark, then spat on the plinth, fouling the carving of the wyvern. He nodded to Miss Aylmer and walked off. Before he reached the edge of the green he turned and shouted back. 'I'll be glad to see that map, when you've pulled it out of the crypt. Let me know if you need a hand.' He gave another amused bark, fitted the key into the gate and went through, swinging it shut behind him with a clang.

'That should tell everyone in the village that you're going to find a map,' said Miss Aylmer. 'What's the next plan?'

Weever was curiously quiet when he replied. 'I really don't know,' he said. 'I didn't think he'd be back. Not after the wyverns chased him off.'

'There's a lot to play for,' said Miss Aylmer. 'He's not giving up easily.'

'And I can't even begin to think how dangerous it will be if he gets the book first.'

'He won't.'

'He may.'

They stood and stared at the gaunt outline of the great house, with the two wyverns clinging to the gateposts.

'They're good friends,' said Weever. 'But they're terrible enemies.'

Thomas could hear his father's low, strong voice. He kicked his boots off on the mat and carried them through the kitchen to the back to dry.

'Get some wood, will you?' asked his father.

Thomas smiled. 'That smells good,' he said.

'Soup,' said his father. Thomas grabbed two logs from a basket and took them through to the one room that served as dining room, sitting room and anything else they needed during the day.

'At least,' he father called through the door, 'it started off as soup. I'll take some up to your mum.'

'I'll do it.'

Mrs Ketch was propped up on pillows, reading.

'Are you all right?' asked Thomas.

'I'm fine. Couldn't be better. Is that soup?'

'Sort of.'

She laughed, dipped her spoon in the bowl and tasted. 'It's delicious, whatever it is.'

Thomas watched her, anxiously.

'I get tired,' she said. 'But I'm lots and lots better. And I'll be less tired the longer I'm home. All right?'

Thomas squeezed her hand. She leaned forward and kissed his cheek.

'Get your soup,' she said.

'All right.' He smiled. 'I'm glad you're back.'

'Eat!'

Thomas settled the logs on the red embers. 'What is it now, then?' he called through to the kitchen.

His father lifted a spoon from the saucepan. 'What do you think?'

'Stew?' suggested Thomas.

'That sounds all right,' said Mr Ketch.

'What did you put in it?'

'Oh, a bit of this and a bit of that. Do you want some bread with it?'

'Please.'

He ladled it into two heavy clay bowls, cut thick slices from a crusty loaf and together they carried them through to the fire. They nestled the bowls on their knees and ate happily.

'What was that you were singing?' asked Thomas.

'I don't rightly know that it's got a name. It's an old song.'

'You haven't sung it before.'

Mr Ketch laughed. 'Well,' he teased. 'I reckon I must have done, or I couldn't sing it now, could I? How's your soup?'

'Best stew I've ever tasted,' said Thomas, honestly.

They ate in silence. The logs shifted as they took the flames.

'Mum said it tasted good,' agreed Thomas.

They settled back into silence.

Small flowers of dust lifted their heads in the fire as the wind swerved round and found ways of darting down the chimney. A fragrant smoke rose from the crackling logs. Mr Ketch rubbed his bread round the sides of his bowl.

'More?' he asked.

'No, thanks. Not just now.'

'It'll keep.'

'Good.'

Mr Ketch put his bowl on the hearth and stretched back in his chair. He hummed a tune lightly. His voice was warm and dark, and carried the tune with the grace and dignity of a solemn procession. Thomas finished his meal in silence, listening.

On the third repetition of the tune Thomas joined in. His own voice was still pure and high. He faltered only once but quickly recovered. The next time he was perfect. They hummed the tune together twice over. Then, when he was sure that Thomas had it perfectly in mind, Mr Ketch let the boy carry the melody while he wandered off, making matching harmonies, sometimes obvious ones which ornamented the main themes, but sometimes making diversions which startled Thomas and made him work hard to keep with the main tune. These were harmonies which seemed sometimes to explain things present in the tune which Thomas had noticed. At other times they seemed to be at war with the tune, not in a harsh, discordant way, but in a complicated and disturbing relationship – just as members of a family may look nothing like each other at first glance, and yet carry something of a resemblance about them which tells the outsider that they belong together.

Slowly, piece by piece, the man unfolded the complex patterns of music he had arranged and then returned to the tune, so that he and Thomas came once more into a unison and finished together.

Thomas stared at his father.

'You've never sung that to me before,' he said.

'No.'

'There were words. When I came in. You were singing words.'

'Shall I teach you those?'

'Where does it come from?'

'It's a Ketch song.'

'What's it for?'

'Listen.'

Thomas waited. His father began to hum, Thomas joined in again, and he held the melody in his clear voice while his father chanted.

> *'There's a blue one.*
> *There's a white one.*
> *There's a nest full of eggs.*
> *There's a spotted one.*
> *There's a speckled one.*
> *There's a nest full of eggs.*
>
> *The mud around the ponds,*
> *And the green tips of wheat.*
> *The flags between the fronds*

Of the ferns as they wait
To unfurl.
In the spring.

There's a big one.
There's a small one.
There's a nest full of eggs.
There's a rough one.
There's a smooth one.
There's a nest full of eggs.

Green shoots on black boughs and
The sun pale as death.
Steam rises from cows and
The cold makes your breath
Smoke out.
For it's spring.

There's a cracked one.
There's a split one.
There's a nest full of eggs.
There's a blackbird.
There's a cuckoo.
There's a nest full of shells.

Strange things come crawling
When the frost grows old.
Sun's fingers start hauling
New life from old.
Watch out.
In the spring.

There's a talon.
There's a bat's wing.
There's a nest full of spells.
There's a barbed tail.
There's a hot mouth.
There's a nest full of worms.

In the spring.
In the spring.

Thomas held the last note with his father, then they let the tune die.

'You've always known about the wyverns, haven't you?' said Thomas.

'I'm a Ketch,' said his father.

'But you didn't tell me.'

'You're not twenty yet,' he said. 'I'm supposed to tell you when you're twenty.'

'Then why now?'

'You made the wyverns fly. I never did that. Nor my father. No one remembers the last time the wyverns flew. But you made them. At Christmas. So it's time to tell you the Ketch things, I reckon.'

'Is there much?'

'Not really. Songs mostly. And mostly it doesn't make sense. Leastways not to me. And it didn't to my father. But you might understand it.'

'Why?'

Mr Ketch clicked his tongue. 'You made them

fly,' he said.

'I don't know how I did it,' said Thomas. 'Perhaps it wasn't me.'

'It's always a Ketch,' said his father.

Thomas thought about this.

'Does anyone else know the songs?' he asked.

'Weever does.'

'And there's a book,' said Thomas hopefully.

'Well, now. There's a song about a book. But there isn't a book. Not a real book. Not that I give you later.'

Thomas showed his disappointment.

'What's the matter, old son?'

'Nothing.'

'You'd best tell me.'

Thomas hesitated. 'We can make things better, can't we?' he asked.

'Go on.'

'I mean people. We can make people better.'

His father sighed. 'I never did,' he admitted. 'They say the Ketch can cure, but I never knew it to happen. Do you think I'd have let your mother lie months in hospital if I could have made her better? If I had a magic book?'

'No,' admitted Thomas. 'But if there was a book, I could maybe use it, even if you can't. I made the wyverns fly. Perhaps, if I had the book I could do it again.'

'You go on then,' said Mr Ketch kindly. 'You find the book.'

'I'm going to,' said Thomas.

'That's the way.'

Thomas grunted. 'Teach me the song,' he said. 'What does it mean?'

'I don't know about that. I can teach you all right. But it means nothing to me. Unless,' he laughed. 'Unless you've to go looking for dragon's eggs in the bushes.'

He began the first verse, slowly, while Thomas repeated it, line by line.

FIVE

It was one of those days that lie to you. The sky was a clear blue, with tiny white clouds. The new green shoots of spring were bright and fresh in the sun. It looked a day to paddle in the pond, to lie in the fields, to throw off your coat, to walk barefoot.

It was a savage day. A day of cruel cold. A whipping-windy, knife-sharp wicked day. A day when the winter ice crept up behind you and

57

attacked without warning, slashing until your knuckles bled, stabbing until your lips split open, and your cheeks and ears were stinging with its whip. It was a lying, deceitful day. It was spring.

Jack looked out of the window and groaned. 'I don't want that,' he complained. 'Look at it out there.'

His mother looked at the sun-washed walls of the Manor and the church.

'I'm looking,' she said. 'But I got the logs in while you were still in bed, and it's bitter out.' She held out Jack's jumper to him again.

Jack pulled it over his head, still grumbling. 'I'll be boiled.'

'We'll see.'

Clare appeared, her legs thick in cord trousers, her body bulging in a home-knitted jumper. 'Wow,' she said. 'Let's get out before I melt.' She tugged on a coat and wrapped a scarf around her head.

'You're mad,' said Jack.

'We'll see,' said their mother.

Clare opened the door. Towser charged through, tongue pink and steaming. The wind sneaked in and troubled the wood ash in the fire grate.

'Shut the door!'

Jack tugged it after him and they had gone.

Mrs Roberts watched them as they ran over to

Thomas's house. Jack put his hands up to his head to protect his ears against the cold. She was waiting for him, scarf in hand when he returned.

'Don't say it,' he said. 'Just don't say it.'

She closed the door and watched him join Clare and Thomas. 'I told you so,' she said to the empty room.

'Where to?' Jack asked Thomas.

Thomas was uneasy. 'I don't want to bother,' he said. 'It's silly. You were right.'

'No I wasn't,' said Jack. 'I've said I'm sorry. I really want to see the wyverns fly again.'

Clare punched him. 'Don't tease,' she said.

'Ow.' Sisters know how to punch. 'I'm not teasing. Honest. I want to make the wyverns fly just as much as you do.'

'I'd rather forget it,' said Thomas. 'Really.'

Clare stared at Thomas, hardly able to believe what she heard.

'But what about the eggs?' she said.

Jack drew his breath in sharply and waited. Thomas could feel Jack's eyes on him. 'Forget it!' he said. 'It's stupid. It's only a game.'

'I know,' said Jack. 'I can show you something.'

'I don't understand you,' Clare shouted at Thomas.

'It's a wyvern,' said Jack. 'Come on. I'll show you.'

Thomas wanted to ignore it, but he couldn't.

'We know where all the wyverns are,' he said.

'Ah,' said Jack. 'You haven't seen this one. Come on.' He ran ahead, hoping that they wouldn't be able to resist.

'All right,' said Thomas. He gripped Clare's arm, very tight. 'No more about the eggs. All right?'

'He wants to help,' said Clare.

'Huh. We'll see. No more. All right?'

'All right.'

They sprinted off after Jack.

Something about Parcel's Stones caught the wind and made it cry out to be free again. Even on a still day there was the suggestion of a sighing. On a windy day the stones moaned and keened.

'Beat you,' shouted Jack as the others approached. He leaned against a tall stone, waiting.

Thomas bit his lips. 'What's going on?'

'I've found a wyvern.'

'Let's see.'

'Come on then.' Jack stepped into the circle.

Thomas hesitated.

Clare waited.

'I'm not going in there,' said Thomas.

'Got to,' said Jack. 'To see the wyvern.'

'Come on,' said Clare. She stepped forward and entered. She stopped, just inside the circle. 'Come on.'

Thomas looked at Jack who was now in the

centre. 'There's nothing in there,' he said.

'It's here.' Jack pointed to the ground.

Clare stepped out again.

'What's the matter?' asked Thomas.

'Nothing.' Clare was holding her head and blinking.

'Are you all right?'

'Just a bit dizzy.'

Towser crouched low to the ground, growling.

'What have you got?' called Thomas.

'Come and see.'

Clare shook her head. 'I'm all right,' she said. She stepped in again, then stumbled, drew back, and pressed herself against a tall stone. She was rigid and frightened. Thomas could no longer see her.

'Where are you?'

'Here,' she called from the other side of the stone. 'Help.'

Thomas was torn between the need to help Clare and his dread of being in the circle.

'Please help,' she said.

Thomas stepped between the stones and felt his head swim. He backed off quickly, banging into the stone. Pressing himself flat against it he closed his eyes and held his breath. His heart was beating fast and he felt so dizzy that he was afraid he might faint, topple forward and fall. He kept his eyes shut and put a hand out, searching the uneven smoothness of the grey stone. He

61

moved his feet in tiny steps, round the stone. At last his hand found Clare. She squealed, then reached out and grasped him. Still keeping his eyes tight shut Thomas moved back, round the stone until he was free of the circle and standing outside. At the last moment, before he broke through the perimeter, he opened his eyes one last time, then dragged himself out and landed on the ground, Clare sprawling on top of him.

Jack was doubled up with laughter.

'You should see yourselves,' he hooted.

Towser licked Clare's face. She put a trembling hand out and stroked him. 'Thanks,' she said.

Thomas was shaking. He sat up and hugged his knees to his chest. It was an effort to keep his eyes open at first, but as he realised that the ground around him was solid he felt more comfortable with them open than closed.

'Did you see it?' he asked Clare, when he was breathing steadily enough to speak.

'I think so.'

'Tell me.'

'We were on top of a cliff?'

'Yes.'

'And it fell away, right in front of us. Down to the sea.'

'Wild. With waves heaving themselves against the rocks.'

'Yes,' said Clare. 'That's right.'

'Did you see a boat?'

'A ship,' said Clare. 'With a huge sail. Going away from us.'

'And a body in it?'

'Yes. A king. Alone. Lying in the ship.'

Thomas sighed. 'That's not so bad then,' he said. 'If you saw it as well.'

They both looked at Jack, standing in the centre of the circle, laughing to himself.

'Sorry I mentioned the eggs,' said Clare.

'That's all right.'

Thomas hesitated. 'Did you see him?'

'Jack?'

'Yes.'

'Yes. I saw him.'

'What was he doing?'

'You saw,' said Clare.

'Tell me. I want you to say it.'

Clare snuggled her face into her scarf, for safety. 'He was flying,' she said.

Thomas gave a deep sigh.

'Is that what you saw?' she asked.

'Yes.'

'Tell me the rest then,' she said.

Thomas looked up, into the circle. Jack was still standing in the centre, balancing on the stone slab.

'He was high above the sea,' said Thomas. 'Riding a wyvern.'

Jack waved at them. 'Come on in,' he shouted. The wind whipped his scarf so that it streamed behind him. 'Come and see.' He pointed to his feet. 'It's a wyvern.'

Clare stood up first and then helped to pull Thomas to his feet.

'Come on,' she said.

Towser followed them yelping round their ankles.

'Here, Towser!' called Jack. 'Stay, boy!'

Towser ignored him.

Jack put out his arms, like wings and bent his knees a little, enjoying the rushing of the wind as it whipped past. He wanted to follow them, but he wanted to stay more. They moved steadily away from him, not looking back. A figure stepped out from the shelter of a stone, behind Jack. It crossed to the centre of the circle and spoke quietly, in its harsh voice. 'That's a good start.'

Jack jumped.

'Oh, it's you again.'

'Who else?'

'You startled me.'

'You'll need stronger nerves than that,' the voice grated.

'Look, I'm not sure about this,' said Jack.

'You saw. You can come in here. Master Ketch can't. He's not the only one with power.'

Jack hesitated. 'They won't trust me now,' he said. 'They saw me come in.'

'They'll have to.' There was a cruel humour in the voice. 'You led them up to the wyvern.'

Jack's eyes lowered to look at the carved figure beneath his feet.

'And they'll want you to tell them about it,' the voice carried on. 'That's your chance. Make them talk to you.'

'They're after eggs,' said Jack, going red in his embarrassment. How could he say they were looking for wyvern's eggs? 'Stupid,' he added, as a preparation.

'Wyvern's eggs.' The eyes lit up.

'Yes,' said Jack. 'Did you know?'

'So, Master Ketch thinks they're laying, does he? You've done well.'

Jack enjoyed feeling important. 'Do you really mean it?'

'Yes. We'll give him eggs.'

'No,' said Jack. 'I mean about power. Have I got power?'

'You're in here, aren't you? Master Ketch can't come in.'

'It's not much, though,' said Jack. 'Just coming in some old stones.'

'Tell Master Ketch that!' snapped the voice, with an edge of cruelty that made Jack gasp.

'Sorry,' he said.

'Oh, you'll do.'

'But I want to make the wyverns fly,' said Jack. 'That's the thing.'

'Why?'

'Because I saw them,' said Jack. 'Because

they're huge and wonderful and, and, and . . . '
his voice trailed off.

'Go on.'

'Because he can,' admitted Jack. 'Because he did it and I want to.'

'We'll need the book, then,' the voice rasped out. 'You help me. If we can get the book we can make the wyverns fly. And then, there'll be no stopping us. But make no mistake, if that vicar and his meddling friend get there first, we're finished. They know about its power. And they're with Thomas Ketch. They won't let us share it. Will you help?'

'I will,' said Jack. 'I'll do anything to get the book.'

'Will you, though? I will.'

Jack shuddered at the determination in the harsh voice.

'Anything,' it repeated. 'Go on, now. And tell them what you've seen.'

'They won't talk to me about it,' said Jack. 'Not after what just happened.'

'They'll talk,' the voice promised. And it laughed.

SIX

Miss Aylmer's harsh voice rang out across the green. 'Terrible wind.'

Mrs Ketch huddled into her coat. 'Cuts you like a knife,' she agreed.

'Feel it more as you get older. I never noticed when I was young.'

'You didn't grow up round here, though,' said Thomas's mother.

Miss Aylmer gave her an amused stare. 'I've

67

lived in America for years, of course,' she seemed to agree. 'But I was here for a while as a child.' She challenged Mrs Ketch to ask more, to seem to pry into her background. All the village wondered about her, but her manner was difficult and her tongue sharp. She turned questions away easily. 'I expect Thomas doesn't feel it. Children don't.'

'In England as a child?' asked Mrs Ketch.

'Yes.'

'Near here?'

'Oh, the snow we had in those days,' said Miss Aylmer. 'Every year, it seemed. And deep.'

'It's not the same now. We don't see snow but one year in ten. Was it far from here?'

'But the springs were no different. Except that the gutters weren't so good as they are now. The water ran off the roofs and then froze before it had time to hit the ground. The icicles. They were as big as swords.'

'That's right,' said Mrs Ketch. 'It's been so long I'd forgotten. I've seen them like spears.'

'Well, I'll be getting on,' Miss Aylmer said. 'I hope you're properly better.'

The voice was just as harsh as ever, but Mrs Ketch was taken aback by the note of concern.

'I'm sorry,' she said. 'You sent me the little wyvern from the Kych Stone. It was kind of you. I never thanked you.'

'No need for thanks,' said Miss Aylmer. 'As

long as you're better.'

'I am. I'm a lot better.'

'Good.'

'The thing is, though. That with a thing like that, you never know.'

'No.'

'They can do a lot. But they can never say, "That's it. You're all better. For ever." Do you know what I mean?'

'We're never all better. Not for ever,' said Miss Aylmer.

'I know. But Thomas thinks . . . '

'He thinks it's all going to be fine for ever.'

'That's right.'

Mrs Ketch hesitated. Then she said, 'Thomas talks to you, doesn't he?'

'Some.'

'What's going on?'

The great iron gate of the Manor squealed. The two women turned their heads. Beneath the stone wyverns gripping the flint gateposts stood a squat, grey man. He fastened the gate, folded his arms and stood looking out over the green, perhaps at them, perhaps at the statue of Jane Gwyer, perhaps just into the grey-green spring morning, where the thin mist sucked the colour out of the landscape. It was impossible to accuse him of staring at them, impossible to ignore him.

'I don't know,' admitted Miss Aylmer.

'Why have you come back here, now?'

69

'I never said I'd been here before.'

'I won't play games with you, Miss Aylmer,' said Mrs Ketch. 'I'm better. But I don't know how long for. I don't want Thomas in trouble. I don't want that man making trouble. What's going on?'

'A struggle.' Felicity looked across at the Manor.

'I'm surprised he's come back,' said Mrs Ketch. 'After the trouble.'

'Parcels come and go in Herpeton. You can't keep them away. Not for long.'

'Why don't people make him leave?'

'How?'

Mrs Ketch nodded.

A door slammed. Jack and Clare raced across the green, banged on Thomas's cottage and tumbled in. Towser nipped through just before the door could trap his fluffy tail.

'Fair enough,' Miss Aylmer agreed. 'Come on in.'

Parcel nodded knowingly as the two women disappeared into Viviper Cottage. He breathed out slowly through his mouth, enjoying the wisps of steam that curled in the air, like smoke from a dragon's jaws. But most of his attention was fixed on the cottage where the three children sat in front of the fire. He cocked his head to one side, like a dog, listening. Then he shrugged, plunged his hands deep into his pockets and set off. He left a damp trail where his boots swept the dew.

Thomas was fiddling with Towser's ears.

'It's all in your mind,' said Jack. 'You could go in if you wanted to.'

'We both felt the same,' said Clare. 'We were high up and it was awful.'

'Giddy,' Thomas corrected her. 'We felt giddy.'

'Like we were high up,' she said.

'Fear,' said Jack.

'Anyway,' said Thomas. 'The point is, what's in there?'

Jack's eyes were bright. 'You'll have to share,' he said.

'What?' Thomas was suspicious.

'Are you looking for eggs?'

'No,' said Clare.

'I'm not telling, then,' said Jack. 'If you're lying.'

'All right,' said Thomas. 'We were going to, but we're not now. It was a game. But this is real.'

'How do you know?'

'I'm a Ketch,' said Thomas. 'We know.'

Jack scowled. 'Anyone can make the wyverns fly!' he said. 'Anyone. If they know the way. I could do it.'

Clare clenched her fists. 'Don't be stupid. You couldn't. You don't even believe in them.'

'All right,' Thomas agreed again. 'You could.

If you knew the way. But you don't, do you?'

'No.'

'You don't want him to,' said Clare. 'Don't help him.'

'I'd rather work together,' said Thomas. 'I can't make them fly either. Remember? We need the book.'

'He hasn't got it.'

'You know what's in the circle, don't you?' said Thomas to Jack. 'We need that.'

Jack sat up, cross-legged in front of the fire. He drew breath. 'It's a stone,' he said. 'The size of,' he paused, thought, 'a dustbin lid.' He drew an imaginary stone on the carpet. 'And there's a wyvern, in flight, carved in it.'

'We need to see it,' said Thomas.

'We can't,' Clare objected.

'I'll show you.' Thomas ran upstairs. Brother and sister glowered at each other.

'I'm watching you,' said Clare. 'Don't you try to cheat us.'

Thomas landed back at the foot of the stairs. 'Here.' He had sheets of white paper, and a knob of grey wax. 'Brass rubbing,' he said. 'Jack can take it into the circle, put it on the stone and get an impression.'

Jack scraped a sliver of wax away with his fingernail. 'What will you do for me?'

'What do you want?'

'The book.'

72

Clare snorted.

'We haven't got the book,' said Thomas.

'When we get it. I want to look at it. Read it for myself. I want to use it.'

'You can't!' said Clare. 'No.'

'Once,' said Thomas. 'No more.'

Jack nodded. 'Once,' he agreed.

'All right.' Thomas put out his hand and they shook on it.

'And the eggs.'

'Yes?'

'If you find any, I want to see them.'

Thomas looked away as he said, 'Yes.' So Jack knew that he had meant it about the book, but that he was lying this time. Thomas would not show him any eggs.

'Come on, then,' said Jack. 'Let's go.'

Thomas felt himself grow giddy again as they approached Parcel's Stones. He drew deep breaths to steady himself, and when Jack ran straight in through the ring of stones he wanted to throw himself to the ground to stop himself falling.

Towser stood at the edge with Thomas and Clare, growling.

'It's too windy,' shouted Jack, struggling with the flapping paper.

'Weigh it down with stones,' said Thomas.

'Right.'

'Try now.'

Jack rubbed the wax energetically over the paper.

'Torn,' he called.

'Doesn't matter,' said Clare. 'Come out.'

'Try another bit,' suggested Thomas. 'Get a good one.'

Jack moved the paper along, started again and rubbed more gently.

'That's better.'

'Come out!' Clare shouted again. Even though she was cross with Jack she still felt anxious for his safety while he was inside the circle.

Jack sprang to his feet, rolling up the paper. He stood upright on the carved stone, arms out. To Thomas it seemed as though the ground around him was falling away and Jack was riding in the air, this time without any wyvern beneath him. He blinked, and the illusion disappeared. Jack was acting the fool on a stone slab in the middle of a stone circle.

'Let's have a look,' said Thomas.

Jack dropped his arms and stood looking out of the circle towards them. Or so it seemed. His eyes were in their direction. But they had a far-away look that made Thomas turn around. Two figures strode towards them, one tall, one not much bigger than Thomas. They both wore long flowing skirts and had hair flying back behind them. Jack tried to hide the paper behind his back.

'What have you got?' boomed the tall one.

'Something secret,' his companion grated out in a harsh voice. 'See, he's hiding it.'

Jack let his hands come forward. 'Protecting it from the wind,' he shouted.

Weever and Miss Aylmer drew alongside Thomas and Clare.

'Are you spying on us?' Thomas demanded.

'Just out for a walk,' said Weever. 'What's he got?'

'Go and have a look,' Thomas taunted him. He was interested to see whether Weever would.

'I don't think so,' said the huge man.

Jack brandished the paper. 'Come and see,' he shouted.

Miss Aylmer stepped forward, beyond the first stone. She stopped, shuddered, stepped forward again. 'I'll come, shall I?' she said.

Jack lowered the paper. 'I'm coming out,' he said.

Miss Aylmer stepped back.

They held the edges of the paper against the sides of a standing stone. Weever held the top, the others put their hands wherever they could around the edge. The wind grabbed at it and tried to wrench it away, making it look as though the wyvern was alive and rippling its wings in flight.

'That's in there?' asked Weever, sharply.

Jack looked at Thomas, who nodded to him.

'Yes,' he said. 'It's a rubbing.'

Weever whistled. 'In the middle?' he asked.

'Yes.'

'What did you see, when you were in there?' asked Miss Aylmer.

Jack looked puzzled. 'Where?'

'All around you.'

'Grass. The stones. A bit of mud.' He laughed. 'No footprints,' he said. 'Of wyverns.'

'Can I keep the torn one?' she asked.

'If you like,' said Thomas. 'But the other one's mine.'

'Mine,' said Jack.

'You can get one whenever you want,' said Thomas, tearing the paper across and rolling up his half. 'This is mine.'

'Huh.' But Jack did not argue.

The children went off, leaving Weever and Miss Aylmer behind, but halfway home Thomas dropped back. 'I'll see you later,' he said. 'Tomorrow.'

'Where are you going?' Jack shouted.

'I need to think.'

'You promised,' Jack yelled. 'Shares.'

'Tomorrow.'

Jack threw the heel of wax after Thomas. Clare trotted after it and picked it up.

'At least he's not going back to talk to them,' said Jack, watching Thomas disappear.

Thomas skirted round the Barrow, missing out

76

the path that would take him back past the Stones. He was breathless when he reached Stone Pond. He doubled up, putting his arms on his thighs and letting his head drop forward, drawing in deep breaths of the cold air. His hair hung down, nearly brushing the muddy fringe of the pond. When his heart had slowed down and his breathing was more comfortable and his eyes were able to focus again, he took one final gulp of air and looked in front of him.

He jerked his head up in his surprise and banged his neck on a low branch. At once, his eyes filled with tears and he was blind again. But he dragged his sleeve across his face and searched the ground beneath the scrubby hedge.

'No,' he whispered. 'I don't believe it.'

SEVEN

Night brought a dry clear sky. The lazy mist which had hung around the village all day, like grief in a house of death, sloped off, leaving the sky full of stars. Out at the back, Mrs Roberts shivered as she finished cleaning down her wheel, checking the temperature on the kiln, and tidying her workshop. 'Sharp frost tonight,' she said, to no one in particular. Then she jumped when a voice answered, 'Skating on the pond, tomorrow.'

'Oh, Jack,' she said. 'Where did you come from?'

'Need some more wood for the fire,' he said.

'Well, close the door after you.' She wiped her hands on her big shirt, switched off the workshop light and went in. 'Do you want a hot drink?' she called.

'Please.' Jack stacked logs in the basket.

The door slammed shut. Behind the windows he could see his mother putting the kettle on to the stove.

Someone coughed quietly at the bottom of the garden. Jack looked up.

'Who's there?'

'Did you put them by the pond?' asked a harsh voice.

'Yes. I made a sort of nest.'

'Good.'

'Are they real?'

There was an evil chuckle. 'Onyx. Got them on a stall in the market in town.'

'He'll know.'

'You didn't.'

'He's a Ketch.'

'Don't you start that, or you'll never make the wyverns fly.'

'What's the point?'

'Point?'

'Of the eggs.'

'Keep him busy. Give us a bit of time to find the book.'

'How?'

'Follow the wyverns.'

'What does that mean?'

'I don't know,' admitted the voice. 'Just let me know anything he says.'

'All right.'

'Especially anything he's seen in the other book.'

'Jack! What are you doing out there?'

'Coming!'

'Anything. No matter how stupid it seems.'

'Jack!'

'Coming!'

'Wyvern Weever
Wyvern Weever
Weever wyvern
Threw the stones.

Fly, wyvern, fly
Through the night.
Darken the sky
With deadly flight.

Wyvern Weever
Wyvern Weever
Weever wyvern
Threw the stones.

Sail, wyvern, sail
Through the sky.
Flourish your tail
As clouds go by.

Wyvern Weever
Wyvern Weever
Weever wyvern
Threw the stones.

Die, wyvern, die.
For ages long
Wait for the cry
Of wyvern song.

Wyvern Weever
Wyvern Weever
Weever wyvern
Threw the stones.

Burn, wyvern, burn
In the deep earth's heart.
Turn, wyvern, turn
When dangers start.

Wyvern Weever
Wyvern Weever
Weever wyvern
Threw the stones.

Wyvern, return
Through ages long,
When we learn
The wyvern song.

Wyvern Weever
Wyvern Weever
Weever wyvern
Threw the stones.'

Thomas listened, entranced. His father's voice carried the melody like a chant.

When the singing was over they sat at opposite sides of the fire, silent.

Thomas's mother knew that she had nothing to do with this. This was Ketch business, and she felt a pang of pain, quite different from the pain that the doctor had cut out in the hospital.

The silence went on for a long time. Then, 'Can I write it down?' asked Thomas.

'We shouldn't,' said Ted Ketch. He looked at his wife. 'We shouldn't sing it at all, when there's others there.'

'You don't mean Mum?' Thomas was angry.

Ted poked the logs in the fire to cover his discomfort. 'It's Ketch business,' he explained. 'We don't write it down. We don't sing it to others. Even wives.'

'That's sexist,' Thomas objected, thinking he was sure he knew what that meant.

Ted was glad of the opportunity to laugh. 'No,'

he said. 'It would be all right if you had a sister. I could sing it to her. It's Ketches that matter, not being a man.'

'I'm going to make some sandwiches,' said Mrs Ketch. She smiled and closed the kitchen door behind her, something she never did.

'I'll sing it again,' said Ted. 'Slowly. Join in when you can.'

And again the man taught Thomas a song.

'I suppose you don't know what this one means, either,' said Thomas.

'That's right. It's the Weever song.'

'I don't like Weever,' said Thomas.

'There's always been Weevers in Herpeton.'

'He's new here.'

'He is, and I've never seen a Weever here before. But that's what my dad said when he taught me the Weever song. "There's always been Weevers in Herpeton." '

'He wants me to teach him things,' said Thomas. 'Should I?'

'You must do as you want,' said his father. 'To tell you the truth, I never thought much of all this. Not until now. I promised my dad I'd teach you the songs. And I made sure you'd promise to teach your children.'

Thomas felt a silly tingle in his neck at the idea of having children of his own. It was about as likely as flying to the moon.

'That's right,' said Ted, spotting the idea in

Thomas's mind. 'That's what I thought. Stupid. But we all grow up. And it seems more important now than it did.'

'Sorry.'

'I'll tell you what, though,' his father added.

'What?'

'The Weevers are worm charmers.'

'Worms,' laughed Thomas.

'Snakes. Slow worms. Vipers.'

'Wyverns,' breathed Thomas quietly.

'It's on the arm,' said his father. 'The wyvern wound.'

'The tattoo?'

'That's right.'

Thomas searched his mind to try to remember where he had seen the tattoo before. On someone else.

'But not like the Ketches,' said Ted.

Thomas returned to the conversation. 'How?'

'They need the book. They had the book, once, and they lost it.'

'How do you know?'

'Listen,' said Ted. 'I'm not supposed to be telling you any of this, yet. Not till you're going to get married.'

Thomas giggled.

'I know. But you made the wyverns fly. And it looks like there's others are trying. So, I'll have to tell you now.'

Thomas wriggled in his chair excitedly.

84

Ted cleared his throat and intoned,

'Thomas Kych has left this tale —
How do the wyverns fly?
Over the Stones, under the Stones.
May I call them up?
As you have my Book, you may call them up.
Shall I do it alone?
Kych alone shall do it alone.
Yet I may have the power?
Call the wyverns if you dare.
How shall I call them up?
Have you drawn the wyvern wound?
Even on my arm it sits.
Read the Book and you will see.
Parcel's Stones stand strong and true,
Ever waiting Wyvern Weever.
Tread the ground with banners bright.
Overhead the wyverns circle.
Nor wake the sleeping king.'

It was like a spell.

'I'll never learn that,' said Thomas.

'Here's a clue,' said his father. 'Just remember the first letter of every line. Then you can't go wrong.' He chanted it again, and Thomas nodded, understanding.

'What is it?'

'It's called "The Weever's Tale". My dad said it meant that Weevers had called up the wyverns, but that they'd lost the secret.'

85

'I wish I knew what that bit means, about throwing stones,' said Thomas.

'Yes. It's a puzzle. I've always thought of it as being like casting, you know, throwing – casting. Like casting a spell. To make the wyverns fly. Perhaps the book has the spell in it, and you have to throw a stone as part of the magic.'

'Yes.'

'But they've lost the book and so they've lost the secret.'

'Sandwiches,' announced Mrs Ketch, pushing open the door. 'Can I come in?'

'The trouble is,' said Thomas, 'we've lost the secret as well.'

'But they're flying again,' said Ted, 'and you made them.'

'Just suppose,' said Thomas.

'Suppose what?'

'Suppose it wasn't me. After all, I didn't mean to. And we know that Weevers have in the past.'

'Then there's Parcel,' said his mother, clinking plates and cups.

'Parcel?'

'The old man at the Manor. He wants to make them fly, doesn't he?'

'I suppose he does,' said Ted.

Thomas clicked his fingers. 'That's it,' he said. 'That's where I've seen the tattoo, the thingy.'

'The wyvern wound,' said Ted.

'That night. In the Manor. He had one on his

arm. That's how he made the vipers stay away from him.'

'Perhaps he made them fly that night,' suggested Mrs Ketch.

'No,' said Ted. 'Doesn't make sense. They chased him away from the Manor. Let the kids go.'

'But remember the Weever's Tale,' said Thomas. ' "Call the wyverns if you dare." Perhaps he can call them, but he can't control them. He needs the book for that.'

'But why should he call them if they're dangerous to him?'

'He didn't know, did he? Not until he tried,' said Thomas. 'See?'

'Hmm. Maybe.' His father wasn't sure.

'Sandwiches,' said Mrs Ketch.

And they agreed.

'Dad,' said Thomas, with an apologetic look at his mother. 'Can I show you something, tomorrow?'

EIGHT

The wind ran around Parcel's Stones, trying to escape. It hurled itself at the circle, moaning and keening.

Weever paced around, like a guard.

Miss Aylmer stood in one place and grimaced at him each time he passed her in his impatient journey.

'What exactly was it like?' he asked her.

'I've told you. Lots of times.'

'Tell me again.'

'Like being very high up, over the sea.' She looked at a piece of paper she held, a photocopy of a page of the old book. 'Delve deep below the wyvern stone,' she read. 'Delve. We thought that meant dig.'

'It does.'

'It can. But look.' She spread out the rubbing Jack had made of the stone. 'That's the wyvern stone.'

'Yes.'

'Does it remind you of anything?'

'A dustbin lid.'

She placed it on the ground and weighed down the edges with stones.

'And now?'

'A manhole cover.' Weever slapped his hand against a standing stone and the wind howled.

'We don't need to dig. We just lift it up. And down we go.'

Weever took her in his arms and hugged her.

'Don't. Someone might see.'

'So what?'

'I don't want them talking about the vicar hugging me.'

Weever roared out a laugh.

'That's the least of our worries. How do we get in there to the wyvern stone?'

'It'll have to be Jack,' she grated out in her harsh voice.

'Will he help us?'

'I think so. If we speak to him properly.'

'At least we don't need an archaeological dig.'

'That was one of your worst ideas,' she said.

'Speaking of that.'

'Yes.'

'There's still Parcel to worry about. We'll have to hide it from him.'

'That's a real problem,' she agreed. She bent to fold up the rubbing, and the wind grabbed the photocopy of the page from the book and whipped it away from her.

Miss Aylmer grabbed. Weever hurled himself forward. Too late. He tottered on the edge of the stones, fell through and toppled over, crashing to the ground inside. He screamed, curled up into a ball, making himself as small as his huge frame would allow, and lay whimpering on the wet earth.

Miss Aylmer, full of dread, closed her eyes, reached out a hand and slithered, like a snake, through the gap, feeling ahead of her, until she could touch Weever.

'Got you,' she said. 'Come on.'

He wriggled and rolled, following her as she backed out of the space. He was sobbing as he reached the safety of the outside. Miss Aylmer did not open her eyes until they were well clear of the stones.

'That was kind of stupid,' she said at last, and

the attack calmed him more quickly than a kind word would have done.

'My stars,' he said. 'Those rocks.'

She nodded.

'And so high above them.'

'Yes.'

The paper was curled around a large stone, inside the circle, held there by the wind.

'We can't leave that there,' said Felicity.

'We can't get it out.'

'Jack can. Let's find him.'

'You try his house. I'll look on the Barrow, round and about.'

It wasn't until they had left the stones out of sight that Weever realised what a stupid mistake he had made. He thundered back, his cloak chasing him.

Felicity was there already.

'One of us should have stayed,' he panted, 'to guard it. Will you, or shall I?'

'It's gone,' she said.

He looked. 'The wind.'

'Let's hope so.'

The flags, the water-irises, whistled stiff and dry about the edge of Stone Pond, their many-knotted stems bent in the wind. The water lapped the muddy sides, and the ripples washed the reeds.

'It's low,' said Ted Ketch. He marked with his

foot the line where the water used to reach. 'Could be a third as big again, if we had the rain we used to have.'

'The snow should have filled it,' said Thomas. 'It was deep.'

'It's helped,' agreed his father. 'But it's not been enough.'

'Through here,' said Thomas.

Ted looked to right and left. The low, morning sun struck the water and both his eyes were dazzled as he stood. He raised a hand to shield them from the glare. 'We're not overlooked?' he asked.

'No,' said Thomas. 'I've been looking. Here.' He stooped forward, brushed aside a branch and revealed the rough nest.

Ted Ketch was silent. He stared down at the clutch of seven green eggs.

Thomas wished he would speak.

Ted slowly knelt in front of the nest, then put out his hand. He paused, looked at Thomas. 'Is it all right to touch them?'

'I don't know.'

'Have you?'

'No.'

'Then I won't.'

'Go on. It's all right.'

'We might drive the wyverns away. Like with birds. If you touch the eggs, the bird won't hatch them.'

'Maybe they don't sit?'

'I won't risk it.'

'It's all right,' insisted Thomas. 'Look.' He knelt beside his father, took an egg and cradled it in his hands.

Ted put out his fingers and stroked it. 'It's smooth.'

The green shell was patterned with swirls and whorls of deeper and lighter greens, like grain in wood. He took it from Thomas, gently.

'I never thought to see one,' he said. 'And so big. I thought it was all stories and songs.'

Thomas took another carefully from the clutch. 'I don't think they sit on them,' he said. 'I think they just hatch out.'

'But where?'

'Where what?'

'Where did the wyverns come from? To lay the eggs.'

'From the gateposts of the Manor.'

'No. That's not right. They haven't flown. Not since Christmas Eve.'

'There must be others. Round here. In secret.'

Ted looked around again, as though the wyverns might come swooping down to protect their brood. 'I suppose,' he agreed. He weighed the egg in his hand. 'Doesn't feel like an egg,' he said. 'Heavy. More like a stone.' He examined it. 'Marble.'

'Marble isn't green.'

Ted thought hard. 'Something is, though,' he said. 'Alabaster? No. Samite? No, that's white, I think. Onyx. That's green.'

'You mean jade,' said Thomas.

'No, onyx, I'm sure.'

They laid the eggs carefully back in the nest.

'But they wouldn't be like birds' eggs, would they?' said Thomas. 'They're wyverns.'

Ted smiled at him. 'I hope you're right. I wouldn't want to get fooled.'

Thomas smiled back. 'No danger of that,' he said. 'I'm the only one that knows they're here.'

'What about your friends?'

Thomas put his hand on Ted's arm. 'I'm not telling them. Not even Clare. I'm leading them on a wild goose chase. To do with Parcel's Stones.' And he told his father about the riddle in the book. 'It doesn't mean anything,' said Thomas. 'I just know it doesn't, but they're all excited about it, Jack and Weever and such. So, I'm going along with it. It won't lead anywhere.'

'Make sure you're right,' Ted warned him.

'I'm right,' said Thomas. 'I'm a Ketch. So, we'll play along with the game, and we'll keep the eggs a secret.' He put the branch back where it could hide the nest. 'Just between ourselves.'

'He's found the eggs,' said the harsh voice.

'Good,' said Jack. 'I made the nest where I knew he'd look. And I made it seem hidden.'

94

'You did well.' Parcel gave him a crooked grin.

'I don't see how he'll ever believe they're real eggs, though,' said Jack. 'They're obviously stone.'

'He believes it,' said Parcel. 'I watched them. They put them back so carefully. And then they hid the place again.'

'What now?' asked Jack.

'Now,' said Parcel, 'you help them to lead us to the book.'

Jack snorted. 'No one knows how to find that.'

'I do,' said Parcel. He unfolded a photocopy of a page of writing.

Jack peered over. 'Where did you get that?'

'It just blew my way,' said Parcel.

Jack read it, his lips moving. 'The wyvern stone?' he said, when he had finished.

'In Parcel's Stones. Exactly,' said the man. 'Now we know where that is, don't we? But they don't.'

'Why?' Jack dreaded the answer.

'Because we've been in the circle, haven't we? And they haven't.' The chuckle was not a pleasant sound. 'They've never seen the wyvern stone. And they won't.'

'What do you think we do?' asked Jack.

'Lift it,' said Parcel. 'And dig.'

'We can't do that.'

'Easy. Just watch me. Or, if you want to use the book, help me.'

Jack's heart was beating so hard it hurt his chest. He did not dare to tell Parcel that he had shown Thomas the wyvern stone, that he had rubbed a copy for him. But if he found out. 'We ought to go there quickly,' he said. 'In case they find out. Do they know about this?' He nodded towards the paper.

'Yes.' Parcel hesitated. 'But they can't understand it.' He glared at Jack. 'Can they?'

'It says, "Delve deep below – in Parcel's Stones." It won't take them long to find a way.'

Parcel swore. 'You're right,' he added to his oath. 'We'll do it soon. You run off, now. I'll tell you when I want you.'

Jack made his way to the end of the brick passage which ran alongside the pub. He glanced quickly up and down the street to make sure he was unobserved. Above his head a wooden board swung on rusty hinges, squeaking mournfully. Jack looked up. A wyvern spread its wings, THE GREEN DRAGON emblazoned beneath. Above the door to his left ran the legend – *L.S. Caton, licensed to sell by retail, beer, wines and spirits for consumption on or off the premises*. A warm smell of smoke and beer drifted into the evening air. Caton himself was away. He had left someone else in charge while he went to somewhere in America – New England, Jack thought he had heard – on a business deal.

The street was empty and Jack stepped out

and sprinted home.

He had nearly made the safety of his front door when Weever stepped out of Viviper Cottage, right in front of him. He swerved to avoid the man, but a huge hand gripped his collar.

'Ah, young Jack the lad. Just the person. Come on in and have a word.'

NINE

The cottage was so hot that Jack felt himself
break out into a sweat. At least, that was what
he told himself. Shakti was coiled beneath the
small table, head raised, tongue flicking. Jack
put himself as far away from the snake as possible.

Three pairs of eyes turned to him as he tugged
off his coat and scarf.

Weever closed the door quietly.

'What's this?' asked Jack. He felt as though he had been brought for trial.

'Planning meeting,' said Miss Aylmer.

'I've got to get home,' said Jack.

'Don't be stupid.'

'All right, Clare,' said Weever. 'He doesn't have to stay.'

'He does,' she insisted. 'He's the only one that can help us get in.'

Jack noticed that Thomas was not saying anything. He decided to tease him.

'I suppose you've found the wyvern's eggs,' he said.

'No,' said Thomas.

Jack stared at him. 'Come again?'

'No,' said Thomas. 'I haven't.'

'What's this?' asked Felicity, sharply. 'Are they laying?'

'Ask him,' said Jack.

'Well?'

Thomas put his hand on his chest. 'I haven't found any.'

'Hand on heart,' Jack mocked him.

Thomas placed his hand on his chest. 'Hand on heart,' he said.

The two boys stared at each other.

'That's not what we're bothered about just now,' said Weever.

Miss Aylmer frowned and looked unsure, but she decided to leave alone the matter of the eggs, for the moment. 'We need to get into Parcel's Stones,' she told Jack.

'You just walk in,' he taunted her.

'No,' she said. 'You can. We can't. And no one else can, either.'

'Is that right?' he said.

'As far as I know,' she said. 'No one ever goes in there. No one ever has. Unless you know different?'

Jack ignored the question. 'Go on,' he said. 'And then what?'

'We're going to trust you,' said Weever. 'So we want you to promise that anything we say will be secret between us.'

Jack placed his hand on his chest. 'Hand on heart,' he said, looking at Thomas.

Weever explained about the page of the book and about the importance of the wyvern stone. 'It's a gate,' he explained. 'The circle lets you into another place. That's why we can't go in. But for some reason, you can.'

'What's it like?' asked Jack, interested at last.

'High up. Above the sea. With waves crashing against the cliffs,' said Felicity.

Thomas and Clare did not mention that they had seen Jack riding the wyvern above the sea.

'Really?' Jack's eyes shone.

'Really,' boomed Weever.

'And I can go there, but you can't,' he said, wonderingly.

'It seems so.'

'So, then, perhaps I'm the one who's to have the book.'

'No,' said Thomas.

'Then why can I go and get it? You can't. I must be meant to go in. Anyone who can get into the circle is meant to have the book. Meant to make the wyverns fly. Meant to have the power.'

'We'll find that out when we've got the book,' said Weever.

'Let's have a look,' said Jack. He took the paper with the riddle on and scanned it, recognising where the photocopy had come from. 'It doesn't say anything about finding the book,' he said.

Weever explained to him that the key was the book.

Jack nodded. 'All right,' he said. 'What do we do?'

Weever clapped his hands together. 'Good. Now we're off. I've got it all worked out.' His thick fingers grasped a pencil and he drew a circle on a scrap of paper. 'Here's the stones. You go in, and you crowbar off the wyvern stone. Then, we might need to dig, but I don't think so. I think there's a passage underneath. We run a ladder from the outside of the circle to the stone. You make it secure your end. Then, we'll cross the ladder to join you and down we go.'

Jack laughed. 'You mean you're going to crawl along the ground on a ladder?'

Clare raised her voice. 'It's not the ground to us. It's high up. Remember?'

'But it isn't,' said Jack. 'It really is the ground. You can see it.'

'If things were always what they looked, then the world would be simpler,' said Felicity.

'What does that mean?' asked Jack, rudely.

She thought. 'All right,' she said. 'I can get you to touch Thomas, without crossing the room to get to him.'

'You can't,' said Jack. 'See.' He reached out his hand. Thomas was metres away. 'There's no way.'

'Yes there is.'

'Show me.'

Felicity took a small looking-glass from the desk. She handed it to Jack. 'Turn it so that you can see Thomas. Now, touch him.'

Jack's fingers brushed the glass. 'It's a cheat,' he said. 'I'm not touching Thomas.'

'You are, and you're not,' she said. 'But there's another way.'

'Go on.'

Felicity took Thomas by the hand and led him to Jack. 'Now touch him,' she said. Jack brushed Thomas away.

'He came to me,' he argued.

'I never said he wouldn't. So, it depends where you look, how you look, and what the other person or place is doing. If they come to you or not.'

Thomas remained standing above Jack.

'Oh, go away,' said Jack. 'I'll do it.'

'Good,' said Weever. 'Tomorrow. First thing.'

'You'll need to get ladders,' said Jack.

'Got them. In the church. We use them for getting up to the roof. And ropes. And spades, if we need to dig.'

Jack shuddered as he thought of what the church would need spades for.

'Five o'clock,' said Felicity.

'That's too early,' Jack argued.

'Got to be done quickly. Parcel's eager,' she said. And she watched Jack carefully. 'And we've got to do it before anyone's about.'

Towser beat his tail against the floor.

'Five o'clock,' said Weever. 'At the church.'

The stone wyverns turned their blind eyes to one another. Jane Gwyer stared blankly into the clear night. And another figure, short, squat and keenly alert, hid in the shadows and watched as the three children left Viviper Cottage, Jack and Clare to their house, Thomas across the green to his.

'And the Weever stays behind,' murmured Parcel from the obscurity of his post. 'Now what's all that about?'

He waited until all was clear, then he made his way behind the cottages, positioned himself at the end of Jack's garden and waited. It was cold, but he did not shiver in his long vigil. When Mrs Roberts came out and filled a basket full of logs he gave up his watch, certain that he would not be able to catch a word with Jack, and he returned to his gate.

The church loomed up against the iron-grey sky. Weever leaned against the carved porch, looking into the dying night. Already, in the east, the trees were visible against the lightening sky, but the Manor and the huddle of cottages were only a suggestion of themselves, still asleep.

A small scuffle from over the green drew Weever's attention. Then there was silence, until Thomas loomed into sight, fronded with early mist.

'Got the stuff?'

'Here.'

One moment they stood in a hostile isolation, the next, Felicity was with them, as if formed from the mist.

'Shall I throw a stone up at Jack's window?' asked Thomas. 'They might have overslept.'

'We're here,' whispered Clare.

Towser rubbed against Thomas's legs.

'If we're quick,' said Jack, 'we'll get there before it's light and you can walk across.'

'We'll take the stuff,' said Weever. 'Just in case.'

Weever carried the ladder. Thomas and Clare carried the long rope between them. Jack carried two shorter ones. Miss Aylmer managed the two spades and a crowbar. Towser did his best to make them drop things.

'See,' said Jack. He hurled the ropes down. 'It's not quite light. Come straight in.'

Weever stepped across the boundary formed by the ring of stones. He yelped and fell back.

'What's up?'

'Falling headlong through the night is no less terrifying than in the daylight, I guess,' said Felicity.

Weever gasped in inarticulate agreement.

'Oh, all right,' said Jack. 'Give us the crowbar.'

Clare gripped Thomas's arm. 'Aren't you nervous?'

'No.'

She shook him. 'Don't be like that. You must be.'

Thomas said, 'I know it's a waste of time.'

'Why?'

'When I looked in the book, I saw that thing, about the wyvern stone. I just knew it didn't mean anything. Jack won't find anything there at all. We'll dig till dinner time, then we'll go home.'

'Why are you here, then?'

Because I want to draw the trail away from the eggs, said Thomas, silently. But he didn't say so. 'They wouldn't do it without me,' he said instead.

'That's true,' she agreed.

Jack struck the wyvern stone with the crowbar and the blow rang out through the dawn.

'Prise it up,' shouted Weever. 'Here,' he encouraged Thomas. 'Get this ladder ready.'

Thomas helped to slide the ladder across the circle.

Jack shoved the curved end of the crowbar along the rim of the wyvern stone.

'It's tight,' he called.

'Push!'

'I am!'

'Tie the ladder to this stone,' said Weever.

It was a difficult job, getting the rope around the monolith without going inside the circle, but with some help from the spade handles they managed.

'Heave!' Weever called to Jack.

Jack, back bent, arms tense, threw his weight on to the crowbar. It grated against the stone, flew free and sent Jack sprawling.

'Again!'

'All right!'

Jack strained harder. The stone groaned and moved upwards a little, then it slipped back.

Weever drew breath to shout again, but Felicity silenced him. 'In his own time,' she said, softly.

This time, Jack managed to fit the crowbar right down the side. He levered efficiently, and the stone lifted. He made an angle with the crowbar and sent the stone swerving off to one side.

'Got it!' he called.

'What's underneath?' demanded Weever.

'Just a minute.' Jack was struggling to get his breath back.

Weever manipulated the other end of the long ladder, to bring it closer to Jack. It landed alongside the wyvern stone, and went several metres beyond it, making a firm bridge.

'I'm coming across!' he called.

'Careful,' warned Felicity.

'Follow me,' he said. He closed his eyes, fell to his face, and slowly crawled along the ladder.

The stone grated as Jack pulled it aside.

'Hey!' he called.

Weever opened his eyes, involuntarily, felt sick with terror at the height and swiftly closed them again. He stopped crawling and waited for his head to clear.

'What is it?' called Clare.

'There's a tunnel.

She punched Thomas. 'See!'

'How deep?' asked Felicity.

'Can't see. It's too dark.'

Weever was moving forward again.

'I've got a torch,' he said. 'Wait.'

His hands found the edge of the opening. He

crawled up to it, leaned over, and put his head in. 'I just hope I can look down this thing,' he said. He found his torch in the folds of his cassock, flicked the switch and opened his eyes.

He was looking down into a tunnel, lined with bricks, like a wall. It went straight down, the height of a tall man, then turned off and fell in a slope, deep into the earth. There was no sign of cliffs, or the sea, or sky, just a round, brick-lined blackness.

'Here we go,' said Weever.

He swung his legs round, disappeared into the hole, feet first, then poked his head back out.

Jack sat on the grass and watched him.

'It's like being in a high, narrow tower,' said Weever. 'Frightening, but not terrifying.'

'But what about me?' said Jack. 'What am I doing?'

'Come on in,' said Weever. 'There's just room.'

Jack squeezed in. 'I'm going down,' he said.

Weever slipped him a torch. 'Only a little way,' he warned. 'Then wait.'

Towser tripped along the ladder like a circus dog on a tightrope. He jumped in and followed Jack. Clare next. She held tight, opened her eyes once, then made the rest of the way with them tight shut.

'It's funny,' she said. 'Although the ladder's flat on the ground, I could feel it swaying in the wind.'

'It's real,' said Weever. 'There's some sort of gate here, into where the wyverns live. And the ladder's on the other side of the gate, so it is swaying.'

Clare wrinkled her nose. 'I don't understand that,' she said. 'But if you say so.' She dropped down after Jack.

Thomas did not even try to open his eyes on the way over. His knuckles were white with the force of his grip, and he came very slowly. Miss Aylmer checked that the rope was secure and followed last. Weever helped Thomas into the tunnel, but Felicity hopped in unaided and lit a small torch.

'I want to go first,' called Thomas.

'First. First. Irst. St,' came the echo.

'Too bad,' Jack shouted back. 'Oobad. Oobad. Bad. Ad.' 'I'm off.' 'Moff. Off.'

It was a tight fit. The tunnel sloped down, sharply at first so that they slid, then with a more gentle slope, until, at last, it levelled off.

'It's very dry,' Felicity observed.

'No rain to speak of for ages,' said Weever.

'I don't think that's why,' she said.

They shuffled along on the level, the ceiling of the tunnel growing higher all the time.

'The bricks have stopped,' Jack told them. 'It's bare wall from here.'

Soon they could stand upright, except for Weever. Then they could walk two abreast.

'Which direction are we going?' asked Clare.

'Towards the Barrow,' said Weever.

'To the buried king,' said Miss Aylmer.

They continued for a while in silence, awed by the idea of finding the ancient burial.

'I wish I'd brought a lantern,' said Weever. 'These torches don't show up everything.'

Felicity opened her cloak and there was a click. 'It's a battery one, I'm afraid,' she apologised. 'I didn't trust oil underground.'

'Why?' asked Clare.

'Gas,' she grated.

'Boom,' laughed Jack.

The lantern showed them the height and width of their passage. It was more a small cave than a tunnel now and they could stand in a circle.

'The floor's still sloping,' said Felicity. 'I think it has been all along.'

'So we're very deep,' said Clare.

'Far deeper than they ever dug their trenches in the Barrow,' said Miss Aylmer. 'It's no wonder they didn't find anything.'

'But shall we?' asked Weever, grimly.

'Not if we stand here,' said Thomas.

Clare squeezed his arm as they set off. 'I thought you said there wasn't anything,' she teased him.

'I was wrong,' he admitted. 'But I don't like it. It doesn't feel right. I still don't think we're on the right track.'

Towser banged his tail against Clare's legs.

'Come on, anyway,' she said. 'Let's see.'

The cave was narrowing again, and growing lower. Weever found it more difficult to keep going.

'What if it's a dead end?' asked Jack.

'Can't be,' said Weever.

But the tunnel grew lower and lower, so that Weever was struggling to get through. And the air grew rank. And the floor grew steeper. It began to twist and wind.

'I've lost my direction,' said Felicity. 'Which way are we going now?'

'Down,' said Weever.

They were in single file again, Jack still leading.

The tunnel turned sharply and Jack stopped suddenly.

'That's it,' he said.

'What?' Weever barked out.

'Dead end.'

'Can't be,' said Clare.

Weever struggled through, pushing the others out of his way, banging his head and swearing softly.

'See,' said Jack. His torch shone against a rock wall. 'Dead end.'

'Told you so,' Thomas whispered to Clare.

'Don't be horrid.'

Weever kicked the stone. It boomed back

at him.

'It's hollow,' he yelled.

He kicked again. The booming echoed round them.

'Stop it,' said Miss Aylmer. 'Show some respect.'

'You'll wake him up,' jeered Jack.

'Nor wake the sleeping king,' chanted Miss Aylmer.

They paused.

Weever brushed the rock. Flakes of dry mould and puffs of dust fell away.

'It's a door,' said Jack. His eager hands helped Weever.

'Can you open it?' asked Clare.

'They'll need a key,' Thomas predicted.

'The key's the other side,' said Weever. 'It's the book.' He could not hide the excitement in his voice. Together, he and Jack scrabbled at the rock door, clearing it of debris.

A pattern emerged beneath their hands – a wyvern, claws poised, flames searing from its jaws.

They stopped and looked.

'What is it?' asked Felicity.

'Wyvern,' said Jack.

'It would be,' said Thomas.

'Here's the edge of the door,' said Weever. He dragged more dust away with his finger ends and revealed a fissure. 'Feel,' he said. Jack put his hand to the crack and felt a rush of cold air.

'We're nearly there,' said Weever. 'See.'

'Hush.'

'What?'

'Listen.'

'What's that?'

They waited. They listened.

Boom. Boom. Boom. A regular pattern of thuds came from the other side of the door.

'Something's moving about in there,' said Clare.

'It can't be.'

'You can hear.'

Between the thuds there was a roaring, like fire being dragged up a chimney.

'We don't have to go in,' said Jack.

'We can't get in,' said Felicity.

Weever applied his shoulder to the door. It moved. He pushed again. With a grating complaint it moved more. The booming grew louder.

'Nor wake the sleeping king,' said Felicity.

'What if we do?' asked Clare.

'We've been warned,' said Thomas.

TEN

The sun was clawing its way over the horizon when Parcel arrived at the circle. It sent fingers of light across the fields and between the tall stones, casting long shadows in mysterious patterns.

Parcel kicked the end of the ladder and snorted.

'That's it, is it?'

He fumbled with the thick rope, tugging at the

knot. He pulled the ladder clear of the circle and made his way to the centre. The wyvern stone lay at a crazy angle, where it had been left by Jack. 'Don't like tunnels,' he said. 'They've done me a turn here.'

The veins stood out on his neck, and the sinews in his thick wrists as he tugged at the stone. At last, it sank back into place with a grind and a sigh. Parcel looked around. Most of the rocks in the circle were quite small, the size of a cricket ball, not much more. Some lesser standing stones were buried, and stood waist-high. But there was one slab, not beneath the ground, balanced against another. This rocked, like a see-saw. Parcel tried to lift it, but it was too much for him. He fastened the rope to its higher end, braced his feet in the soft earth and tugged. He slipped a little, but the swivelling action of the angle made the stone slip more. He tugged harder. The stone rocked, swerved, grumbled a protest, and fell, half on, half off the wyvern stone.

Parcel found his eyes had blurred and there was a thudding in his head, but when he could see clearly again he was delighted. The great rocking stone had toppled just where he had hoped. No one would lift the wyvern stone from beneath now. In fact, he wasn't sure he could move the rocking stone. He folded his arms, tired but pleased. The thudding in his head started up again. No. Wait. He put his head in his hands and took a deep breath. His eyes were clear. He was no longer dizzy. Still the thudding. Boom. Boom. Boom. He sat down on the rocking stone and felt the thudding come up through his legs. He touched the wyvern stone. It thrilled beneath his fingers. Boom. Boom. Boom.

'Well, now. I'm glad I'm not down there.'

'Give me the crowbar,' said Weever. 'We'll soon have this open.'

'There's something in there,' said Jack. 'Let's go back.'

Weever took the iron bar and jammed the curved end in the crack of the door.

'Listen,' said Jack.

'I can hear all right,' said Weever.

Felicity put out her hand to calm Jack's fears. Her cloak fell away from her arm. 'You can stand at the back if you want.'

Jack stared at the arm, ghostly white in the light of the battery lantern.

'You're the same,' he said.

On the woman's white arm writhed a tattoo of a purple snake.

'The wyvern wound,' said Thomas.

Weever stopped pulling at the crowbar. 'You know that as well?'

'Everything,' said Thomas.

'Then what's behind this door?'

'Nothing,' said Thomas.

116

Jack yelped in disbelief. 'Nothing! You hear that thudding! And that roaring! That's fire, that is. That's wyvern fire. I'm getting out of here.' He shouldered his way to the back of the group and along the tunnel. 'Come on!' he called. 'If you go through that door they'll get us all.'

'Go on, then, coward,' Clare shouted.

Jack hesitated, but he did not return, afraid to stay, ashamed to leave.

'Well?' asked Thomas.

Weever and Miss Aylmer waited.

'What now?' Thomas continued.

'We go in,' said Felicity.

'And charm the wyvern?' he asked.

'Yes,' said Weever.

Thomas smiled. 'But you can't,' he said. 'You need the book to do that.'

'The book's in there,' said Weever. 'I know it is.'

'So's the wyvern,' said Thomas. 'Listen. It won't let you get the book.'

'You can charm the wyvern,' said Felicity. 'Without the book.'

'I could,' said Thomas. 'If I knew how.'

Clare joined in. 'So we can't go in,' she said, 'without the book. And we can't get the book unless we go in.'

'That's right,' said Thomas. 'So let's go back. Jack's right.'

Clare stared at him in astonishment. 'You

don't mean it?'

'Yes,' said Thomas.

'He means it,' said Weever. 'He doesn't want anyone to have the book.'

'Why not?'

Weever wagged a long finger at Thomas. 'You think you'll learn, don't you? How to charm them. You don't want the book found. I've worked it out. It's a danger to you, if we find the book.'

Thomas stuck his hands in his pockets. 'You'll be killed if you open that door.'

Weever turned, seized the crowbar and gave it a mighty pull. The door swung open, wide enough to let them pass. 'We'll see,' said Weever.

Boom. Boom. Boom. The thudding was louder than ever. Jack hugged the wall.

Weever hesitated, and Felicity sprang past him and through the door. He yelled, dived in after her and they were gone.

'Come on,' said Clare.

Thomas hesitated.

'Oh!' she shouted. 'You're as bad as Jack,' and she slipped through the door.

Thomas followed, cautiously.

Weever stood, arms upraised, hair streaming back in a strong wind, his cassock billowing out behind him. Thomas could see the purple tattoo of the wyvern wound on the man's thick arm. It was as though the drawing in the book had come to life. And, as in the drawing, over his head flew a wyvern, golden eye burning in the lantern light.

The wyvern swooped down, and Weever ducked. The fierce talons scraped the air above the tall man's head. Boom. Without turning, it flew back and hissed above him again. Boom.

Weever shouted out something in a language Thomas could not understand. He leaped to his feet again, arms outstretched. The wyvern swooped again. Again Weever ducked just in time to avoid being torn to pieces by the sharp claws. Boom.

The wyvern flew back. Boom.

Thomas darted forward, threw himself at the man and sent him tumbling over.

'Look!' he shouted.

Weever gazed up at the wyvern. It flew overhead again. Boom. Then back. Boom. Making no attempt to follow him, always describing the same course.

The roaring was loud in their ears, like a wild fire.

Felicity and Clare were pressed against the far wall. Towser leaped up pointlessly at the serpent as it flew above him.

'It's not real,' said Weever.

'No,' Thomas agreed. 'But it could still kill you.'

The great bronze wyvern hung on a bar from

a pivot, at the other end of which was a counter-weight. It swung backwards and forwards; and as it reached the end of its flight the great bronze ball of the counter-weight struck a gong, booming out its deep-throated warning.

Felicity and Clare edged their way towards the others.

'It's only dangerous as you come in,' said Felicity. 'It can't follow you. But you're in its path when you step through. I dodged.'

'And I ducked,' said Weever.

'And I stepped round you,' said Clare.

'What started it?' asked Thomas. 'It can't have been doing that for thousands of years.'

'The wings,' said Felicity.

'How?'

'Didn't you feel the draught when he broke the seal around the door?'

'Yes.'

'That must have let the air circulate. There must be another opening for it somewhere, but it can't rush through as long as the door's sealed.'

'I see.'

'The wings act like a kite. And the bang of the counter-weight on the gongs keeps it swinging.'

They watched it, marvelling at its beauty and deadliness.

'The claws are knives,' said Thomas.

'I can see that,' said Weever, drily.

'And it must be hundreds,' said Felicity,

'not thousands.'

'What's that?' asked Thomas.

'The tunnel. The door. This wyvern. They're hundreds of years old. Not thousands. Someone built this, connected the Barrow and the circle.'

'What for?' asked Weever.

'I don't know. But they wanted to keep people out.'

Only Clare bothered to look around her. The others seemed hypnotised by the bronze wyvern. She tugged gently at Weever's sleeve, and said, in a soft voice, 'The buried king.'

The wyvern flew in a great cave, the ceiling beyond the reach of the lantern's light. At the far end from the stone door loomed a long ship, its prow disappearing into the darkness.

Weever turned his eyes towards it.

'Now that,' said Miss Aylmer, 'is the real thing. They built the tunnel to get to that.'

'Who did?' asked Thomas.

'Do you need to ask?'

'Thomas Kych?'

'I guess so.'

Weever gripped her arm. 'The key,' he said. 'We've found the key.'

'Where?' asked Thomas.

'In the timbers of the buried ship. That's where the book is. We're there. We can just walk across and take Thomas Kych's book.'

'My book,' said Thomas.

Weever set off.

The ship was secured in a cutting in the rock side of the cave, holding it upright, as though at sea. Like a giant insect with stiff legs, it carried oars for its last voyage. Weever mounted the wall, then stepped forward and on to the broad deck. It creaked and complained beneath him.

'Careful,' said Felicity. 'You'll fall through.'

Thomas hopped on after him. 'It's very firm,' he said.

'Dry, in here,' said Weever. 'And the timbers are oak, by the look of it, soaked in pitch to preserve them.'

'It's not possible,' said Felicity, when she stood beside them. 'So strong and sound.'

'A boat to go on forever,' said Weever. 'On your last journey.'

'It's a wyvern,' said Thomas.

The stern of the boat tapered off to a curved tail, barbed at the end. They moved to the prow and held the lantern high. The sides drew together, then rose into a curved neck, ending in a wide head, jaws gaping, wooden carved flames curling from its mouth.

Thomas had a sudden memory of Jack, perched on a wyvern's back, flying high above the waves and out to sea. With a sick feeling he felt the brush of death's cloak, knew that one day he would ride that wyvern, that Jack would really fly off on the dragon's back, that his mum would

take her turn on . . . But he stopped there, too
dizzy to let the thought live. He looked around,
urgently, wanting to fix his attention on something, anything.

Clare was stooped over a pile of blankets.

'The king,' she said.

As she drew back, the others saw that the
jumble of cloth was not a blanket or a sail, but
the robed body of a shrunken figure.

She stood, ashamed that she had been so
casual in her approach.

'I'm sorry,' she said.

Thomas felt the brush of the cloak again. They
were already aboard the wyvern. They were
sharing the king's last journey.

Weever knelt. 'Where's the book?' he demanded. 'It must be here.'

'Clovis!' snapped Felicity. 'Where's your
respect?'

He backed away.

'It's what we came for,' he argued.

'To rob the dead?'

'No.'

'Then beware.'

Weever ground his teeth impatiently. 'What
shall we do?'

'We'll not rob this king,' she said.

Weever had disturbed the robes. Miss Aylmer
stooped and tried to put them straight again. As
she tugged at the patterned cloth it crumbled in

her hand.

Boom. Boom. Boom. The incessant noise of the wyvern was casting up clouds of dust. The intrusive reverberations of the air in the cave were fracturing and destroying the patterns of over a thousand years. As they looked, the shape of the king shifted, leaned to one side, and slid away, crumbling into dust. The large bones of the body; part of the skull, the pelvis, one knee, remained, but the rest ran down like sand in an hourglass.

Weever groaned.

'It wasn't you,' said Felicity. 'Don't worry. It was the noise of the wyvern.'

'It's not that,' said Weever. 'Look.'

They watched the heap of dust that had once been a king. Weever put his hand into it. Clare shuddered. He moved aside a helmet, took up the remains of what had been a leather glove, studded with bronze, removed a bracelet, coiled round like a snake. Other artefacts he ignored. 'See,' he said. 'There's no book here.'

'I'm not surprised,' said Thomas.

Weever glared at him.

'Thomas said,' said Clare. 'He said the book wasn't in here.'

'It crumbled,' said Weever. 'It's turned to dust.' He could barely conceal his anger.

'Perhaps,' said Felicity, 'but I think not.'

'No?' Weever snatched eagerly at a small ray of hope.

'Take the key from the timbers of the buried ship,' she said. 'Let's look for a key. In the timbers.'

'Wait,' said Thomas. 'The booming. It's stopped.'

'Good,' said Weever.

'He's right,' said Felicity. 'It shouldn't. The draught's still there.'

Weever was searching the timbers, ignoring Miss Aylmer.

The wyvern had slowed down and was swinging clumsily on its pivot. It began to move from side to side.

'The hinge is giving way,' said Felicity. 'Quickly.'

'We're all right,' said Weever.

'No, it's going to crash.'

'Good.' He ran his hands over the boarding of the deck, looking for an opening, a door, a secret panel.

'If it falls,' she warned in a threatening voice, 'who knows what a row it will make, or what will crumble next.'

'The roof could fall in,' said Clare.

'Out! Now!' snapped Miss Aylmer.

The wyvern began to cry as it skewed over on the breaking hinge.

'We can't!' shouted Weever.

'Got it!' yelled Thomas. He snatched a key from a hook on the mast and brandished it in front of

Weever. The man made a grab for it but Thomas was too quick. He leaped over the side of the boat and sprinted for the door.

Weever growled. He had to go the longer way round, by the wall, not risking landing heavily with his great weight. Miss Aylmer followed him. Clare jumped after Thomas. Towser was at the door before any of them.

'Run for it!' screamed Felicity. 'We're there!'

A terrible rumbling and roaring filled the cavern. The wyvern crashed to the ground and lay mortally wounded, its wide mouth gaping in a dying agony as the tumbling ceiling cascaded down, making a pitiful death song which wrenched at Thomas's heart and beat inside his head. He turned to take a last look at the dying bronze beast, but Weever ducked his head, scooped the boy up in his arms and swung him out of the cave, just as the roof crashed down, burying the ship, the wyvern and the king for the last time.

'And very nearly you, too,' gasped Weever as he slammed out through the door and put Thomas down. Clare was gasping for breath in the choking dust that came through the gaps round the door. The force of the blast had swung the stone shut behind them. Towser licked Thomas's face.

'All right,' said Felicity. 'That won't have done the tunnel much good. Let's go.'

Small trickles of dust, falling from the roof of the tunnel, like the trails of sand in an hourglass, confirmed what she said about the roof fall weakening the tunnel. Weever dragged Thomas to his feet. 'I wish the roof was higher,' he grumbled. 'Still, we'll be out in a couple of minutes.'

'No we won't,' said a small voice.

Clare flicked her torch ahead and its beam caught the white face of her brother.

'I've tried,' he said. 'The stone's across the opening. We're trapped.'

ELEVEN

'I'll lift it,' promised Weever. 'Don't you fear.'

'You'd better,' said Felicity. She put a slender finger to the roof of the tunnel. Small cracks were appearing.

'Like eggs breaking,' said Thomas.

Weever ducked his head, let his arms swing loose by his sides and he ran along the tunnel. His broad back sometimes cracked into the ceiling, but he made no sound, no cry of pain or protest, and he led them at a brisk pace along and up.

'My legs,' groaned Thomas. 'I'm going to fall.'

'Think of mine,' snapped Weever. The man's long legs were bent nearly double in his crouch. He had the skirts of his cassock bundled up and he held them in his hand.

The journey back seemed more than twice as long as their descent to the cave of the buried king.

'Did you find anything?' Jack hissed to Clare.

'No,' she lied.

'You did.'

'Shut up and run.'

Towser loved it. He ran through their legs and round and back.

A sudden crash behind them made Weever stop. Thomas bumped into him. Weever rested his hands on his broad hips and gasped for air.

'What was that?' said Jack.

'Roof,' said Felicity. 'The tunnel's falling in.'

Dust swept up to them. They turned and set off again.

'Bricks again,' said Clare. 'We're nearly there.'

Weever ran straight into the wall at the end of the tunnel.

'We are there,' confirmed Thomas.

'Here we go.' Weever stood, legs just bent at the knees, back against the bricks, arms and shoulders poised to lift. He strained. He ground his teeth with effort. He pushed.

'Nothing,' said Felicity.

'It's not that heavy,' he complained. 'One more heave.' He pushed and pushed, then sank to the floor, rubbing his eyes to clear the dizziness.

'Try again,' laughed a grating voice.

They looked up.

'Or are you tired out?'

'Parcel?' yelled Thomas.

'Mr Parcel to you, Master Ketch.' Parcel laughed, a harsh, grating noise.

'You can't hold the stone down,' shouted Clare.

'What a lot of you there are down there,' said Parcel. 'Why don't you all push?' He was enjoying it.

Felicity put her head close to Weever and said quietly, 'We haven't got a lot of time. The whole thing's going to fall in.'

'What do you want?' asked Weever.

'That's better. Much better. I want the book.'

'We haven't got it,' said Weever. 'There's nothing down here.'

'Nothing?'

'Just a tunnel. It doesn't lead anywhere. Dead end.'

'That's enough!' The mocking humour had gone from the man's voice. He snapped at Weever. 'Give me the book.'

'There's nothing. There never was.'

'Delve deep below the wyvern stone far from

Stone Pond – in Parcel's Stones – Take the key from the timbers of the buried ship. My Stones. My ship. My key!' he shouted. 'The book. Give it to me.'

Weever sank down. 'He knows,' he said. 'We missed the book. It's in there somewhere, and we missed it. He won't let us out.'

Thomas produced the heavy key he had snatched from the mast. 'It's not a book,' he said. 'It's a *key*.'

Towser had stopped prancing about and was huddled against Thomas's legs.

'What's up, boy?' murmured Clare.

'He knows the tunnel's about to go,' said Felicity. 'He can sense it. We're nearly out of time.'

Weever took the key and shook it in silent fury up at the stone above his head.

'Give it to him,' said Thomas. 'It's not important.'

'It is important,' Clare argued. 'You can't.'

'We need it,' said Weever. 'Wherever the book is, we need this key to get it. Don't you see?'

'Your mother,' said Felicity. 'How will she be, if Parcel gets the book?'

Thomas closed his eyes. 'Give him the key,' he said. 'We don't need it.'

Weever shouted. 'There's no book!'

'Liar!'

'There's a key, but no book.'

'Jack?'

131

All heads turned to Jack.

'Jack!' he shouted again. 'You there?'

'Yes.'

'Is it true?'

Jack nodded.

'He can't see you,' said Felicity.

'There's a key,' said Jack. 'No book.'

'You take the key.'

Weever held it out grimly.

'Got it?'

'Yes.'

The noise behind them in the tunnel had grown so loud they could hardly hear Parcel lever the rock from the stone. Then there was a grating noise and a small crack appeared. Fresh air rushed in.

'Push the key through,' came a voice, harsher even than the stones rubbing.

Jack fed the key through the crack.

'Quickly,' said Felicity.

Weever pushed Jack aside and shouldered the stone away swiftly. Then he picked up Jack and tossed him out.

'Make the ladder steady for us,' he said.

'It isn't here.'

Weever did not stop to think. 'Close your eyes and crawl out,' he said. Thomas struggled, but Weever tossed him after Jack. Then Clare. Felicity argued but he ignored her and lifted her high and tossed her free. She landed in an undignified heap of long skirt. Towser was next, and he sped straight off. Weever closed his eyes and jumped up. He felt a sick feeling in his stomach as he jumped free of the hole, then he stumbled, banged his knee against a rock and opened his eyes in pain.

Felicity's eyes were tight shut as she tried to straighten her skirts. Clare was crawling blindly towards the edge of the stones. Thomas had curled into a ball and was just beginning to get his breath back before he too could crawl away. Jack had sprinted to the ladder and was tugging it to the centre. Towser scouted around, looking for a trail to take him to Parcel, but finding nothing. They were all on solid earth.

'Open your eyes,' Weever called. 'It's all right.'

Felicity squinted. Clare blinked. Thomas curled up tight again and tried a peep. Slowly they opened their eyes properly, stood up and looked round.

'It's gone,' said Thomas.

'The gate's closed,' said Weever. He stood, tall in the circle.

Felicity stood next to him. 'One less opportunity,' she said.

Jack dropped the ladder and joined them.

Thomas was the last to stand. 'I can't see it any more,' he said. 'But I can still sort of feel it. Like being high up.'

'Less opportunity for what?' asked Clare.

133

'You were working with him,' said Weever to Jack.

'Not really.'

'What then?'

'He gave me a chance,' said Jack.

'Chance to what?' asked Thomas.

'To be someone,' said Jack. 'Like you are. To charm the wyverns.'

'Less opportunity to break through,' said Felicity.

'To what?' asked Clare.

'Is that what you really want?' asked Thomas.

'It's what we all want, isn't it?' said Weever.

'But why?' asked Thomas.

'I don't know,' said Felicity. 'An opportunity to break through into the past perhaps, when wyverns flew.'

'I want to charm them so that I can use them for something,' said Weever.

'I want to make them obey me,' said Jack.

'You want them because your mum will be all right if you can charm them,' said Clare. 'That's the best reason.'

'No,' said Thomas.

'It is,' she argued.

'Let him speak,' said Felicity.

'I want them to fly,' said Thomas, 'for the sake of it. Just so they can.'

'That's the best reason of all,' said Felicity.

'I want Mum to be all right as well,' he

added, hurriedly.

Jack put out his hand. 'I'm sorry,' he said. Again.

'Whose side are you on?' he asked.

Jack's hand waited. 'I'm on my side,' he said.

'Parcel's?'

'Not any more.'

Thomas took Jack's hand and shook it. Again.

'What will he do now?' he asked Weever.

'He'll look for something for the key to fit,' he said.

'That won't be easy.'

'No. But one of us will find it. And we need to have the key back.'

'It might not fit anything,' said Clare.

'It fits something,' said Felicity. 'And it's time it was opened. The gates are closing.'

'He'd better be careful,' said Thomas. 'He might not like what he finds when he turns the key.'

'What do you mean?' asked Weever, sharply.

'I don't know.'

'What *do* you know?' asked Miss Aylmer.

'Nothing.'

'Thomas,' said Jack.

'Yes.'

'The eggs.'

'Eggs?'

'You know.'

'No.'

'I put them there.'

'What?' Thomas went white.

'He gave them me. They're stone. Onyx.'

'No.'

'He bought them in the market.'

'I don't believe you.'

Jack put his hand in his pocket and drew out a stone egg. 'Here. I kept one.'

'No,' said Thomas.

Jack swung his arm and threw the egg against a stone. It shattered. 'See?' he said. 'I'm sorry.'

Thomas turned and ran. He did not look back.

'You pig!' said Clare.

'Yes,' said Jack.

'He wasn't bothered about the key, or the book,' she said.

'No,' Weever agreed. 'I wondered about that.'

'Because he had the eggs,' she said. 'He was sure his mum would be all right because of the eggs.'

'Yes.'

'Oh, you pig,' said Clare again. 'See what you've done.'

'I'm sorry,' said Jack again. 'What will he do?'

'If the wyverns don't fly, what will happen to his mum?' asked Clare.

'The doctors are making her better,' said Weever.

'Maybe,' grated Miss Aylmer's voice. 'But maybe he needs the wyverns to make it work.'

They looked at the earth beneath their feet and the silent ring of grey stones.

'You can't keep it up for ever,' said Ted Ketch.

Thomas looked up, startled. 'Eh?'

'You'll have to talk to us sometime,' he said, with a smile.

'Sorry. I was miles away.'

'Where?' asked his mother softly.

'I don't know,' said Thomas. 'High up.' And he told them, at last, about the circle and the wyvern stone.

Mrs Ketch hugged herself as he told it, as though she was cold. The fire was deep red with heat.

'And it's closed now?' she asked.

'Yes. Closed for ever, I think.'

'Nothing's for ever,' said Ted.

'Some things are,' she corrected him, gently.

'Yes.'

Thomas wanted to hug her, but he was too old. 'You're still not properly better,' he said.

'Mostly,' she said.

'I want you all better. I thought if the wyverns flew you would be.'

'They still might,' said Ted. And he gave Thomas a knowing look.

'Jack put them there,' he said. 'They're not eggs at all. They're stone.'

Ted nodded.

'I'll get rid of them tomorrow,' said Thomas.

Mrs Ketch drew the curtains against the darkness outside.

'I don't need the wyverns to fly,' she said. 'I'm getting better anyway.'

Thomas smiled, unconvincingly.

'I can make them fly,' offered Ted.

'Get on with you,' she smiled.

'Listen.' He put his hands on his knees, stared into the fire and began to sing softly.

'Riding the clouds on a pointed perch
The wyvern runs to the east.
In chain mail scale astride the church
She leaps and lopes — the gleaming beast
To ride the wind.

When the wind sweeps round to the evening west,
She twists with a silent scream,
And she soars and plunges through to test
Her strength against the rushing stream
And ride the wind.

Leaping high to chase the north
The wyvern snakes her tail,
To lash the wind as it drives her forth
Like a Viking boat with rounded sail
To ride the wind.

She lifts her nose to scent the breeze
That brings sweet rest from the south.
The wyvern's wings sweep back with ease,
As she stretches up with laughing mouth
To ride the wind.'

There was a long silence.

'I shouldn't be listening to this,' said Mrs Ketch at last. 'It's against the rules.'

'We're changing the rules,' said Thomas.

'Can you do that?' She smiled.

'I don't see why not,' said Ted. He sang again. Then Thomas tried. Mrs Ketch hummed gently, following the tune, not attempting a harmony. Her voice was pure and pitched just below Thomas's. Ted joined in her wordless accompaniment while Thomas carried the words.

Just once, Thomas faltered and Ted gently corrected him.

'Does it have to be exact?' asked Mrs Ketch.

'Every word, perfect,' said Ted.

Thomas tried again. This time he made no mistakes, and the words flowed smoothly, with the insistent humming of his mother and father carrying him along. They finished with a snap, not letting the last note drag on.

Thomas nodded. 'I've got that one,' he said.

'Right.'

They watched the fire. The wind whined, whipped round to another direction, then dropped suddenly.

Ted raised a corner of the curtain and faced the darkness. 'It's turned,' he said. 'Calm tomorrow. Warmer.'

'Spring,' said Mrs Ketch. 'Flower spring. Not frost spring any more.'

'I'll shift those eggs in the morning,' said Thomas.

TWELVE

Parcel mocked them as they passed his gate. He brandished the key. 'I win,' he said.

'It's not over yet,' said Ted. He strode up to the gate and Parcel backed away hurriedly.

'Leave him, Ted,' said Mrs Ketch. Her face was drawn and she seemed to be in pain.

Parcel barked out a harsh laugh.

Thomas took her hand.

'That's it, Master Ketch. Cling to Mummy.' He

141

waved the key again.

Thomas detached himself and turned to Parcel. 'Be careful, Parcel,' he said. 'You may unlock something you can't control with that key.'

Parcel contorted his face in what was perhaps anger, perhaps fear.

They did not look at him.

'Why did you say that?' asked Ted, when they were out of Parcel's hearing.

'We're not looking for a key. We're looking for a book.'

Mrs Ketch squeezed his hand.

'You're not better, are you?' said Thomas.

'I thought I was, last night. When we sang. But it comes and goes. I'm getting better.'

Thomas hung his head. 'I'll make you better,' he said. 'When I get the book.'

'When the wyverns fly,' she said.

'Yes.'

'But he's got the key,' said Ted.

'It's not over yet,' Thomas repeated his father's words to Parcel.

'That's true, but it's a setback.'

Stone Pond shone in the warm, spring sun. The flags bent in the breeze. Thomas dragged aside a branch and revealed the tangled ring of nest that branched itself, fine as frost ferns on January panes. Seven eggs huddled tight in the centre.

'They're lovely,' said Mrs Ketch.

'But useless,' said a deep voice.

Thomas stepped back and saw Weever and Miss Aylmer.

'What are you doing here?' he demanded.

'Don't be rude, Thomas,' said his mother.

'Same as you,' said Weever. 'Looking at the stone eggs.'

'They look like the real thing,' said Felicity.

Weever put his hand out to lift one.

'Don't touch!'

'Thomas!' said his mother.

'Sorry.'

Weever's arm hovered over the nest. A bracelet circled his wrist, a coiled snake.

'That's from the buried king,' said Thomas. 'You stole it.'

Weever withdrew his arm.

'What will you do with them?' asked Miss Aylmer.

'Throw them in the pond,' said Thomas.

'Seems a waste,' said Weever. 'They'll be expensive. We could take one each. A souvenir.'

'No!'

'Throw them in the pond,' agreed Ted. 'Best place for them.'

'Isn't there an egg song?' asked Miss Aylmer, innocently.

Thomas looked at her sharply.

'What do you know about that?'

'I'm not rightly sure,' she said. 'Is there?'

'It's Ketch business,' said Thomas.

'All the same,' she said. 'I think I'd sing it, if I were you.'

'Why?'

'Seems the thing to,' she said. 'What with the eggs, and all.'

'Not with him here,' said Thomas, pointing to Weever.

Mrs Ketch was tired of telling him off, so she stopped herself from saying 'Thomas!' again.

Weever roared with laughter.

'You stole the book,' said Thomas. 'And the bracelet. You'll steal our songs.'

Weever nodded. 'Throw them in, then,' he said.

'You sing,' said Ted to Thomas. 'I'll throw them in. It doesn't matter about the song. He won't tell.'

They stood over the nest. Thomas cleared his throat. The low sun caught in his eyes and he squinted over the pond. He hummed, to get the note right, then started.

> *'There's a blue one.*
> *There's a white one.*
> *There's a nest full of eggs.*
> *There's a spotted one.*
> *There's a speckled one.*
> *There's a nest full of eggs.*

144

The mud around the ponds,
And the green tips of wheat.
The flags between the fronds
Of the ferns as they wait
To unfurl.
In the spring.'

Thomas screwed his eyes up against the sun.
Black dots were troubling his vision.

'There's a big one.
There's a small one.
There's a nest full of eggs.
There's a rough one.
There's a smooth one.
There's a nest full of eggs.'

Beneath the song he could hear a scratching,
like rats in the wall. The black dots grew bigger
in the sky.

'Thomas,' said his mother. He ignored her.

'Green shoots on black boughs and
The sun pale as death.
Steam rises from cows and
The cold makes your breath
Smoke out.
For it's spring.'

Someone pulled Thomas away. He stumbled and
carried on singing. Beating in the air above him,
and hot breath and the smell of burning. The

scratching was louder, cracking, tearing.

> 'There's a cracked one.
> There's a split one.
> There's a nest full of eggs.
> There's a blackbird.
> There's a cuckoo.
> There's a nest full of shells.'

The water at the pond's edge splashed and steamed. Thomas turned his eyes from the sun and saw the eggs, split open, the tiny wyverns struggling out, the two huge serpents, watching, waiting, not helping them.

> 'Strange things come crawling
> When the frost grows old.
> Sun's fingers start hauling
> New life from old.
> Watch out.
> In the spring.'

The heat from the parents' breath was scorching the flags. The tiny wyverns twisted and wriggled their way free from their shells. They were full-formed and perfect, scales gleaming, wings wet at first but drying to leather in the spring air. One opened its mouth, coughed, and a puff of smoke and a tongue of fire licked out. It blinked, coughed again and scurried out of the nest.

146

'There's a talon.
There's a bat's wing.
There's a nest full of spells.
There's a barbed tail.
There's a hot mouth.
There's a nest full of worms.'

Just one egg remained intact. Thomas begged it to crack, to open, to release its wyvern. He sang on, hoping. Six small wyverns waited. The huge parents spread their wings, dragged barbed tails through the water and rose up. The babies beat tiny wings, fluttered for a moment, then they were up and off.

'In the spring.
In the spring.'

The last notes died. Thomas watched the wyverns rise up, parents first, babies after them, strung out like a skein of geese. They circled the pond once, dipped, rose again, turned to the east and flew into the sun.

The silence that followed seemed deeper than the night sky.

Mrs Ketch raised an arm to wave farewell to the wyverns. She smiled. 'Look,' she said quietly to Thomas. 'It doesn't hurt when I lift it.'

'Really?'

'Really.'

Weever whistled.

'You knew,' said Thomas to Miss Aylmer. 'Didn't you?'

'What shall we do with this last egg?' she asked.

'Leave it. It might hatch,' said Weever.

'No,' she said. 'It won't.'

Thomas stooped and picked it up.

'It's yours,' said Weever. 'A keepsake.'

'You don't know anything, do you?' said Thomas. He lifted it, weighed it in his hands and flung it into the pond.

'No!' shouted Weever. Too late.

The egg splashed into the water, sank and hit the bottom with a clunk.

'That's odd,' said Ted.

'What?'

'That noise. You'd think there was mud down there.'

'They flew again,' said Mrs Ketch. 'I saw them.'

'I made them,' said Thomas.

'How?'

'They just came for the babies,' said Weever. 'It wasn't you.'

'I feel so well,' said Mrs Ketch. 'So well.'

Ted Ketch took her hand. 'That's grand,' he said. He looked around. 'We've done well today.'

'Yes,' agreed Weever.

Towser hurled himself at Thomas's legs.

'Hush,' said Thomas.

'Hello!' called Jack. 'What are you all doing

here?' He looked a little ashamed.

'What about you?' demanded Weever.

Jack dived into the bushes about a third of the way round the pond from where they stood. He dragged out a clumsy nest with five eggs in it. 'Came to get rid of this,' he said.

'Stupid,' said Clare. 'I don't know why you ever – '

'All right,' he agreed. 'I'm sorry. Here.' He gave a stone egg to Thomas. 'Souvenir.'

Weever took one, gave it to Felicity and took another for himself.

'I reckon I'll have one as well,' said Ted.

'Not for me,' said Mrs Ketch. 'I'm done with dragon's eggs for today.'

'Just the one left for you,' said Weever to Jack.

Jack took the egg and flung the nest into the pond, where it floated, aimlessly.

'So,' he said. 'We're back where we started.'

'Not quite,' said Weever. 'Not quite. But there's more to come.'

'I reckon,' agreed Ted.

Thomas raised his head, screwed his eyes up against the pale, spring sun. 'But they flew,' he said. 'They flew.'

And they all looked to the east.

Some Other Puffins

A HANDFUL OF THIEVES
Nina Bawden

Set a thief to catch a thief!

There were five of them – which is why they were called a handful of thieves. Not that they were real thieves, of course. They just had to act like thieves to catch the sinister Mr Gribble.

He pretended to be just an ordinary lodger, but Sid knew better. Apart from anything else, it wasn't right for a tall, thin man like him to talk with a voice like that!

So when Gribble scarpered with Gran's savings, Sid wasn't surprised. But he was determined to get the money back – even if it did mean the five children had to behave themselves!

BAGTHORPES UNLIMITED
Helen Cresswell

'I want a family reunion.'

Grandma Bagthorpe should have realized the consequences of such a momentous announcement. Chaos and disaster are inevitable on the arrival of Uncle Claud, his boring wife and their two horribly clever children. Soon it becomes clear that they will have to be driven out – which means even more pandemonium in the crazy Bagthorpe household.

BINGO BROWN AND THE LANGUAGE OF LOVE
Betsy Byars

Bingo Brown has a notebook. There are two headings
in the notebook. One says 'Trials of Today' and the
other says 'Triumphs of Today'. And it's the list of
'Trials' that's growing.

Bingo had promised himself he'd give up burning
questions for the summer. But it just doesn't look as if
it's going to be possible. How can he keep up his
romance with Melissa by phone when he's forbidden to
make long-distance calls? How (aged eleven and eleven-
twelfths) can he be expected to handle adult problems?
And is that really a moustache above his upper lip just
waiting to burst out?

AN ENEMY AT GREEN KNOWE
Lucy M. Boston

Strange things are always happening at Green Knowe!

'The queer thing about Granny's stories,' Tolly explained to Ping, 'is that bits of them keep coming true now, although they are all so old.'

This particular story was about Dr Vogel, who had stayed at Green Knowe hundreds of years ago, and had delved further into black magic than he ought.

BLACK JACK
Leon Garfield

Bartholomew Dorking . . . stood almost dead of terror. 'Alive!' he moaned. 'He's alive!'

More dreadful than violent death itself was this reviving from it. A deep rattling sigh filled the room. Black Jack's chest heaved – and his box cracked ominously. His moon-filled eyes rolled fiercely at Bartholomew.

Suddenly the young apprentice finds his life tangled up with a murderous villain. Drawn into the seamiest and most treacherous parts of London, Tolly's wild story involves a private madhouse and a lonely girl called Belle, who isn't really mad at all . . .

THE THREE <u>INVESTIGATORS</u>
"We Investigate Anything"

*

Jupiter Jones, Founder
*

Pete Crenshaw, Associate
*

Bob Andrews, Associate

The Three Investigators
Crimebusters
available in Armada

1 Hot Wheels
2 Murder to Go
3 Rough Stuff
4 Funny Business
5 An Ear for Danger
6 Hollywood Horror

THE THREE INVESTIGATORS ™

6

Hollywood Horror

Megan Stine and H. William Stine
based on characters created by Robert Arthur

Armada

First published in the U.S.A in 1989
by Random House, Inc.
First published in Great Britain in 1990 in Armada

Armada is an imprint of the Children's Division, part of
the Collins Publishing Group, 8 Grafton Street,
London W1X 3LA

Printed and bound in Great Britain by William Collins Sons
& Co. Ltd, Glasgow

1

Thrills and Chills

PETE CRENSHAW PULLED HIS CAR TO THE SIDE OF the road. The small orange 1977 Vega bounced along the uneven shoulder and then stopped right across the street from a cemetery. Pete set the brake, checked his reddish-brown hair in the rear-view mirror, and slid smoothly out from behind the cramped wheel. Not a bad move for a 6-foot 1-inch, 190-pound jock, Pete thought with a grin.

Outside he quickly unlocked his trunk, reached in, and lifted out an arm. It was a long, hairy, heavy arm with smooth muscles like a body builder's. But at the end, instead of a hand, there was a paw. The paw flopped up and down with the motion of Pete's steps as he started across the street.

But suddenly Pete stopped and glanced at his watch. Nine o'clock. Uh-oh. He was supposed to meet Jupe an hour ago.

Maybe there was time for a quick phone call. But was there a phone somewhere? Yeah—a few hundred yards down the road in an old deserted gas station.

Pete hiked to the phone booth, still carrying the arm. Then he slipped a quarter into the slot and dialed a number. After two rings a familiar voice answered.

"Three Investigators. Jupiter Jones speaking."

"Jupe, It's Pete. I've been trying to call you all morning."

"I know," Jupiter said.

I know. Those were Jupiter Jones's two favorite words.

"How can you possibly know?" Pete asked. "You forgot to turn on the answering machine and I've been getting no answer all morning."

"I didn't forget. The answering machine is fried because I blew out all the fuses in the workshop. It's definitely time to convert to circuit breakers," Jupe answered. "And besides, I know because I can logically deduce what happened. You're late, so something important must have come up."

Pete could picture Jupe perfectly—sitting at an old metal office desk in the converted mobile home trailer that the Three Investigators used as their office. The trailer sat near the corner of Jupe's uncle's junkyard in Rocky Beach, California, just up the coast from Los Angeles. Jupe was probably leaning back in the swivel chair, working at his computer—or maybe reading a diet book.

"Okay, you're right, as usual. Something did come up. But it's not just important—it's monumental. Guess where I am?" Pete asked. But he didn't give Jupe a chance to answer, just in case somehow he could. "I'm at Dalton Cemetery down near Huntington Beach, and I've got the special-effects arm my dad has been working on for the new Suffocation movie— *The Suffocation II.*"

"Hmmm," Jupiter said.

"And I'm taking the arm to Jon Travis, the director, in about two minutes. And not only that, my dad thinks Travis may even give me a job. Is this cool or what?"

"It's cool, but be careful," Jupiter said.

"What's that supposed to mean?"

"It means a lot of strange things happened on the first Suffocation movie."

"Like what?" Pete asked,

But before Jupiter could answer, Pete's quarter dropped down into the telephone.

"Talk to you later," Jupiter said. "I *know* you don't have another quarter." Jupe hung up.

Okay. The guy's smart. I'll give you that, Pete told himself as he walked back to the cemetery. Otherwise he wouldn't be the leader of The Three Investigators. But how'd he know I didn't have any more change? And what did he mean, strange things happened on the first Suffocation film?

Pete crossed the road and walked down a grassy slope into the cemetery. When he was a kid, grave-yards used to freak him out. But not now, and not this one. This one was crawling with life.

At the bottom of the first slope there was a level place cluttered with gravestones. Then the hill sloped down again, and the cemetery continued down, down to the bottom of a deep valley. The film crew was set up at the very bottom. Small groups of spectators lined the crests of the hills overlooking the action below.

As he passed through the crowd of onlookers, Pete

saw two high school girls who looked as if they were about his age—seventeen. One of them was watching the film crew through binoculars. "What are they doing now?" the other girl asked.

"They're still digging a grave and just talking," answered the girl with the binoculars.

"Do you see him yet? Is Diller Rourke down there?" asked the other girl. "I'll croak if I don't see him. He has such totally awesome eyes."

"Calm down, Cassie. You're losing it."

Pete laughed to himself. Haven't they ever seen a movie being made? he wondered. Probably not. And certainly not a movie starring Diller Rourke, Hollywood's newest hunk superstar. Not everyone's dad was in the movie business and able to get his kid onto sets.

Pete walked down the next two hills into the shooting area, dodging around lighting equipment and crew members and open graves. *The Suffocation II* was going to be a really weird movie, that was for sure. It was about a guy who accidentally gets buried alive and when he finally escapes from his coffin, he realizes he's turned into a zombie. Class A scream-and-bleed, Pete thought to himself.

At the very bottom of the valley he found thirty-eight-year-old Jon Travis, director of *The Suffocation II*. He was sitting on a canvas chair with his feet up on a huge tombstone, talking into a portable telephone. His black turtleneck and black pants matched his long, greased black hair. At 5 feet 8 inches, Travis was a good five inches shorter than Pete.

"Okay, angel. Where is Diller Rourke?" Jon Travis

yelled into the phone. "Where is our wonder boy megastar, the one you promised me would be on time and know his lines every day?" He listened to the answer at the other end and curled his lips. "You're his agent! That's why I expect you to know. He's held up shooting for two hours! Do you want me to tear his heart out with my bare hands? Get him here!" With that, Travis threw the phone at a young woman with a long red ponytail who was standing nearby.

Travis is everything Dad said he would be, Pete thought to himself. Hotheaded, self-centered, and demanding. Maybe that's what made him such a good director of horror movies. Or maybe it was just because his movies were so bloody and gross. His last movie, *Mondo Grosso*, had been a big hit.

"Margo, keep trying his beach house," Jon called to the girl with the red ponytail. Then the director noticed Pete. "What's that? A back-scratcher?"

Pete gave Jon the hairy arm. "I'm Pete Crenshaw. This is the arm my dad's been working on for you for the coffin scene. He said to tell you that when you burn the arm, the skin will peel in three layers. First a flesh layer, then a green layer with warts, and then a red layer with all the veins and arteries."

Jon looked at the arm and smiled for the first time. "It's sensational. It's perfect! Your father's the best special-effects man I know. He thinks like I do. Why just make something bleed when you can make it bleed *and* blister?" He handed the arm to a production assistant. "Hey, why aren't you in school?" he asked Pete.

"No school today. Special teachers' meeting," Pete explained.

"Yeah, yeah, yeah. Spare me the details. Listen, your dad's been saying you know cars. Is that true?"

Pete nodded.

"Okay. I dreamed up a new idea for a car scene a couple nights ago, but I need someone good to pull it off fast. Are you in the ballpark?"

Pete nodded. "I've got a friend, Ty Cassey," Pete said. "Between the two of us, we can practically make a car talk."

"I don't want this car to talk," Jon said. "This baby's got to bleed—can you handle that?"

Pete nodded again.

"It's got to bleed from the windshield washers," Jon went on. "If it looks like ketchup oozing—it's wrong, you're a wiener, and you blew it. It's got to gush out in waves—as if someone sliced *this* artery."

As he said it he jabbed a spot on Pete's neck. A chill went down Pete's spine.

"Your heart would keep pumping the blood out—*ka-thonk, ka-thonk*," Jon said. "A lot at first, then not so much. It's got to look that way and if you can't do it, tell me now and get out of my sight."

"What kind of car?" Pete asked calmly.

"A Jaguar XJ6, of course," Jon said. "Ever go out and pay forty-five thousand dollars for a car?"

Pete tried to look cool. He didn't want to admit that he'd never paid more than $750 for any car he'd owned.

"I can handle it," Pete said.

"Okay, you're gone," Jon said. "We made a deal with Exclusive Cars in Hollywood. You just tell them what you want and they'll give you the keys. Be back on Monday." He immediately turned back to Margo with the mobile phone.

"Diller Rourke's phone is still busy, Mr. Travis," she said.

Jon grabbed the phone out of her hands and threw it down. Then he turned to another one of his assistants. "Take my car, Kevin. You and Margo go get Diller. Malibu Court. Use force if necessary. No little punk star is going to take his phone off the hook and keep me waiting."

"Right away, Jon," said Kevin, adjusting his gold wire-rimmed glasses. "Malibu Court—is that on the south side of the beach highway or the north?"

Jon Travis glared at Kevin without saying a word. He looked like he was going to jump on him and bite his throat out.

"I know where it is," Pete said. "I live just down the Coast Highway from Malibu in Rocky Beach." Hey, for a chance to meet a cool star like Diller Rourke, I'd even buy one of those stupid maps to the stars' houses, he thought.

"Okay, mechanic," Travis said. "Maybe you can get my star into high gear." He quickly wrote the address on a piece of paper and told Pete, "Take these two out to Diller's beach house and bring him back. If you get lost, keep on going. I don't want to know from you." Travis motioned Pete and the assistants away with a sweep of his hand.

As they got into Travis's red Mercedes 560 SEL, Pete breathed in the smell of the soft, rich leather. Margo and Kevin talked shop in the front seat, but Pete tuned the conversation out. He was having too much fun sinking deep into the leather back seat, becoming a part of it. He was like another accessory in the beautiful, powerful car—and the car had a lot of accessories. Three-line telephone, TV, videocassette player, 200-watt amp with Dolby sound, small refrigerator—the Mercedes was packed. Too bad they were only driving an hour or so to Malibu and not to Indiana.

When they reached the small beach area along the Pacific coast, Kevin slowed down.

"I could definitely live here," Margo said as they passed by the beach houses of the rich and famous.

"Which way now?" Kevin asked Pete.

"Turn left," Pete said.

A mile or so later they pulled up to Diller Rourke's house. It was a single-story building of cedar wood and glass. In the front yard, among the typical California ice plants, there were a lot of highway signs, road markers, and directional signs, which were obviously stolen property.

Margo and Kevin got to the door first and rang the bell. Pete hung back a little. Now that they were here, he felt weird about meeting a big star. What was he supposed to say to him anyway? Hi—you're a cool dude? How come you're making a horror movie when adventure thrillers are really your thing—is it just for the money? No way. Maybe they could talk about cars or something on the way back to the cemetery.

Kevin kept ringing the bell, but there was no answer. Then Margo pounded on the door. Neither method worked. She and Kevin looked at each other with concern.

Finally Kevin tried the doorknob and was surprised when the door opened easily. He hesitated before pushing it wide open. "Yo, Diller!" he called, leaning into the doorway. Still no answer.

As Kevin and Margo disappeared into the house, Pete came closer. What was going on? He heard one more "Yo, Diller!" from inside the house, and then it was quiet—too quiet. Pete's radar turned on automatically. Something was wrong. Quickly he walked through the door of Diller Rourke's house—and stopped cold.

Inside, Pete's eyes swept the living room. The house looked as though it had been turned upside down. All the furniture was kicked over, the tall standing lamps and the plants knocked down. A weird sculpture of four feet coming out of one leg lay on its side. Almost everything that could be broken was smashed to bits and scattered from one end of the room to the other. It looked like there'd been a fight. It looked like a scene out of a weird movie. But it was real—too real.

Margo and Kevin were just standing in the middle of the room, not moving. Pete took one look at them and realized they didn't know what to do next. They were shocked and they were scared.

"What happened?" Margo finally asked.

"I think we'd better check out the other rooms," Pete said.

"Why?" asked Kevin.

"What are we looking for?" Margo asked, still in a daze.

Pete looked around the totally destroyed room again and his face grew deadly serious. "Try a body," he said.

2

Hollywood Hi-Jinx

"Y OU REALLY MEAN IT ABOUT FINDING A BODY, OR are you trying to be funny?" Margo asked.

Pete didn't answer. All he knew was that something was wrong here. His heart was jumping on a trampoline. And he couldn't breathe. This place needed more air. He felt lightheaded.

"Let's look around," Pete said finally, shaking his head to clear it.

Glass crunched under Pete's hightops. He could hardly step anywhere in the living room without stepping on broken glass. He walked through the house, being careful not to disturb the overturned chairs and lamps and other evidence of violence.

What happened here? Pete thought as he walked into Diller's bedroom. The phone was off the hook. That explained the busy signal.

"Diller's not here. Do you think the house was robbed?" Margo asked, coming up behind Pete. "I mean, maybe Diller walked in while the guy was still in the house."

"I don't know," Pete said. "A thief usually tosses all the drawers and closets. He doesn't knock over furniture. Does it look to you like anything was stolen?"

Margo opened a couple of drawers in a tall chest. "Nothing's even been touched," she said.

"How do you know so much about thieves?" Kevin asked Pete.

I'm a detective, Pete wanted to say. But he stopped himself. *Does Jupe think I'm really a detective?* Pete wondered. *No, Pete's great for climbing in a window or knocking someone down. But that's about it.*

"I think we should go," Margo said.

"Not yet, okay?" Pete said, walking back through the living room. *Crunch, crunch.*

Come on, Pete, he told himself. *The broken glass. There's a clue here and you're missing it. Where did all the glass come from?*

Just then Pete remembered something Jupe said often during his many lectures on finding clues: If you can't figure out what's broken, look at what's *not* broken.

It sounded crazy, but so did most things Jupiter Jones said—until they turned out to be right 98 percent of the time. So Pete checked out the kitchen first. He opened the cabinets and looked at all the glasses.

"Hey," Kevin said, grabbing Pete's shoulder, "if you're thinking about taking a souvenir, forget it."

"I'm just trying to figure out where the broken glass came from," Pete said.

Kevin backed off with an apologetic look on his face. "Sorry, man. Tense scene."

All the glasses seemed to be there—none of them broken. Next Pete checked the windows. None broken. Forget the vases, too. There were no flowers or spilled water on the floor.

No clues. No matter how many times Pete walked through the house. Nothing made sense. If Jupe were here, Pete thought, he'd have five theories by now. But, hey—Jupe wasn't the only detective. And wouldn't Jupiter Jones be amazed if Pete Crenshaw solved this case by himself? Bob Andrews too. Though the third member of the Investigators was hardly around anymore, now that he'd gotten a part-time job with a rock music agent.

Driving back to the cemetery, Pete didn't say much. He just listened as Margo and Kevin discussed their theories of why Diller was gone. According to them, Diller left the house before it was destroyed, or he walked away from a fight, or he got drunk and tore up his house and then spent the night in a motel.

After a while Pete shut them out. If he was going to solve this case on his own, he'd have to come up with his own theories. But at the moment Pete didn't have any.

"Hey, am I going the right way?" Kevin asked, looking at Pete in the rear-view mirror.

"That's the first question I can answer," Pete said with a laugh. "No. Take a right onto the highway and head south."

At the cemetery Pete, Kevin, and Margo found Jon Travis standing in a freshly dug grave, telling an actor how to shovel dirt on him.

Standing nearby was an older man who was bronzed and lean, probably from hours on the tennis court. He was wearing white pants and a peach-colored polo shirt that emphasized his suntan and his silver hair even more.

"Back empty-handed? Where's Diller?" Jon Travis asked.

"Could we talk to you privately?" Pete asked, looking down into the grave at the director.

Travis scrambled out of the grave and walked away from the crowd with Pete, Kevin, and Margo. The tan, silver-haired man followed closely behind. Suddenly he wrapped an arm around Pete's shoulder. "I'm Marty Morningbaum, the producer for *The Suffocation II*. You know, I sign the checks and make sure Travis doesn't spend it all in one place. So if you have something important to say, don't forget I want to hear it too." His voice sounded like everyone's favorite uncle.

"Diller wasn't there," Pete said.

Marty Morningbaum looked at Pete, concerned. Pete tried to move away but Marty had a Velcro-tight grip on his shoulder. Something was beeping in Pete's ear. He realized it was Marty Morningbaum's wrist watch alarm. "You're trying to worry me, aren't you," Marty said. "Why? My hair is already gray. Who are you?"

"That's Crenshaw's kid," Jon cut in.

"Diller's house is a total wreck," Margo said. "There must have been a fight or something."

"A fight?" Jon laughed. "Diller doesn't fight. He wouldn't even squash a fly at a picnic—the little wimp. He's only tough on film."

"Well, maybe someone else was fighting in Diller's house and Diller was out," Marty said. "He could be anywhere—shopping, windsurfing. Think logically. We're making a horror movie—not living one."

"That's exactly right, Mr. Morningbaum," Kevin added. "All we really know for sure is that Diller wasn't there, he left his phone off the hook, and he hasn't been home for a few hours."

"He hasn't been home all night," Pete said. Everyone looked at him with surprise.

"How do you know?" Margo asked.

"We were in his bedroom. Didn't you see his bed? It hadn't been slept in," Pete said.

"Very clever. You're smart like your dad, I'm sure," Marty Morningbaum said. "Well, these are very strange goings on."

Hey, Pete thought to himself, maybe I'm not such a bad detective—even without Jupe.

"Mr. Morningbaum, maybe I can help you find Diller," Pete offered. "My friends and I are detectives. We've solved a lot of mysteries. . . ." He handed one of the Investigators' business cards to the producer.

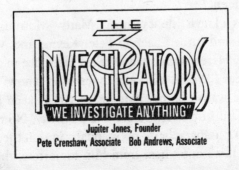

THE
3
INVESTIGATORS
"WE INVESTIGATE ANYTHING"
Jupiter Jones, Founder
Pete Crenshaw, Associate   Bob Andrews, Associate

"The Three Investigators?" the producer said, smiling. "No, no, no. That isn't necessary. Diller may be *gone*, but he's not *missing* until we wait twenty-four hours. That's what the police would say, and they're right."

"Twenty-four hours? Marty, you mean that little glitter-teeth jerk is going to cost us a whole shooting day?" Jon grumbled. "Hey! I've got a great idea. I'm going to shoot a scene where a zombie rips someone's heart out."

"It's not in the script, Jon," Marty said patiently.

"So what? Look—the light is perfect. The crew is in place. We've got gallons of blood, and gore is what people want to see," Jon argued.

"It's not in the script, so it's not in the budget," Marty argued back in a singsong voice.

"Marty, my contract says *I'm* the director, right? You can't take away my artistic control."

Before Marty could answer, Jon Travis took off in the direction of the waiting crew. As he left he turned around long enough to tell Pete, "Don't forget about my bleeding car, Crenshaw! I want a green Jaguar—dark green."

After Travis disappeared, Marty Morningbaum smiled and turned back to Pete, Kevin, and Margo. "Okay. Here's some straight talk." He spoke in a deep whisper. "We're the only ones who know Diller Rourke wasn't home. And we've got to keep it that way. This film doesn't need bad publicity. No reporters, no photographers, no scandal. So don't feed my ulcer. If we don't hear from him tomorrow, then it's serious and we'll do whatever has to be done. Okay?"

"No problem here," Margo said.

"I'm with you," agreed Kevin.

"Okay," Pete said reluctantly. He hated to pass up the chance to work on a good mystery—especially on his own. And his instincts told him this *was* a good mystery.

"Deal," the producer said. He shook Pete's hand. "You've just made a deal with Marty Morningbaum. You ask anyone in Hollywood. It's worth gold."

Okay, so they weren't supposed to talk about Diller being gone. But that didn't mean Pete had to head back to Rocky Beach right away. He decided to hang around and listen to what people were talking about. Maybe someone had some gossip about Diller that would provide a useful clue.

Pete found a group of technical people taking their lunch break. He sat down off to the side, out of sight behind a tombstone.

"Looks like macho boy's a total no-show," said a crew member wearing coveralls. "Rumors are slithering that no one knows where he is. Looks like we trucked out here for nothing."

"Well, it figures things would go kablooey on this film," said another man who was chewing on a piece of red licorice.

"What's that supposed to mean, Ben?"

"Oh, that's right, you guys weren't on the first Suffocation film," said Ben, dangling the licorice out of the corner of his mouth.

"So?" his companions asked.

"Things happened," Ben said. "It wasn't just one of those scream-and-bleed movies. That film was jinxed."

"Like how?" asked the man in coveralls.

"Every time we tried to film the buried-alive scene, the director just suddenly lost his voice. I mean, completely. And that was Roger Carlin, a *real* director. Not a low-budget schlock artist like Travis. That's why Carlin wouldn't touch this sequel. And Corey Stevens, the star of *Suffocation*, got some kind of nervous disease right after the final shooting day. He was sick for a year. And I'll tell you something. I couldn't breathe right the whole time we were shooting. I could go on, boys."

"Hey, things happen on every film," said a young woman carpenter.

"Not like that film. It was jinxed—no two ways about it. And now this one's starting, too."

Pete had heard enough—enough to give him the creeps. He moved to a different row of graves and sat with his back against a tombstone. Beatles songs were coming from someone's cassette player somewhere across the graveyard.

Okay, Pete told himself. Here's what would happen if Jupe and Bob were here. First Bob would tell us what Beatles song that is and which album it's on. And then he'd explain why his boss, Sax Sendler, always tells the bands that work for him to listen to the Beatles. And Jupe would be saying Pete, calm down, take deep breaths, and keep your eyes wide open. There's no such thing as a jinx.

But they're not here, Pete thought, and today I'm handling this case. *Me!*

Suddenly the sun went behind some clouds, leaving Pete in the shade. Then he realized it wasn't a cloud. It was something standing over him and blocking the sun.

"You are very troubled," said the figure. With the sun behind him the man seemed to have a halo surrounding his entire body. He was tall and in his forties. His blond hair was short on top and shoulder length in back. His clothing was all white and loose-fitting—more like pajamas than a shirt and pants. And he was wearing a number of belts, necklaces, and bracelets, each containing crystals of different colors.

"Sometimes it's best not to fight a wave but to let it wash over you." As the man spoke again he sat down facing Pete, cross-legged on the grass. He held out both of his hands to shake Pete's. "Marble Ackbourne-Smith," he said.

"Pete Crenshaw. Are you an actor?"

The man laughed, but it was a happy laugh, not a mean one. "My full-time occupation is to become myself. Not another character. And what about you? How are you connected to this starmania?"

"I'm working on a c—" No, Pete thought, don't say "case." That was close. "I'm working on a car for Jon Travis."

Marble Ackbourne-Smith fingered a long, pointed, pinkish crystal that hung on a silver chain around his neck. "You are concerned about someone in this movie and you have come to a decision crossroads. Which way to go?" Marble was quiet for a moment.

Pete stared at Marble. That's amazing, Pete thought. He knows just how I feel.

"The answer is simple. Don't go anywhere," said Marble. "That is the fastest way of getting to your destination."

Pete was beginning to feel confused. Where did this guy get these ideas, anyway? From Chinese fortune cookies?

Marble Ackbourne-Smith slipped the silver necklace with its sparkling crystal off his neck. He tried to hand it to Pete.

"No, thanks," Pete said. "I'm not into jewelry."

"It's not jewelry," Marble said. "Take it. Talk to it and it will become tuned to your vibrations." Marble slipped the crystal off the chain and closed Pete's hand on it. He stood up to leave. "Listen to it. Listen to the crystal. When I did, it told me there is only one person on this set you should worry about . . . and that person is *you*."

"Hey, wait a minute!" Pete said. "What's that supposed to mean? Is it some kind of a warning, or a threat, or what?"

Pete tried to sound extra tough so that Marble wouldn't see that he was starting to breathe hard. It was the same as in Diller's house—a feeling like being locked in a small closet where someone was sucking out all the fresh air faster than Pete could breathe it in.

"What do I mean?" Marble asked. "I cannot mean anything. I can only say what my third eye sees."

For a moment Pete wondered if the guy was speaking English. "Look, I just asked a simple question. Am I in some kind of danger?"

"Ask the crystal," Marble said, walking away.

Pete opened his hand and looked at the pinkish stone. Sunlight glinted off it and suddenly it felt like it was burning Pete's hand. Pete jumped to his feet and ran for his car.

3

Pumping Blood

PETE HEADED BACK TOWARD HIS CAR IN A DAZE. SO much had happened—too much. And it was hard to sort it all out alone. Could he really handle a case on his own? He wasn't so sure right now.

As he left the cemetery Pete saw Jon Travis strangling an actress. He was showing her how he wanted her to struggle for breath and then finally die. It gave Pete a chill to see how intense Travis looked. Like he wasn't just acting. Like he was really capable of murder.

Pete checked his watch and decided it was too late to worry about Jon Travis's Jaguar today. Tomorrow— Saturday—would be car-shopping day. So he drove home and hid out in his bedroom, dodging all phone calls. He didn't want to talk to Jupe or Bob—not until he was ready to tell them what was going on. And he didn't even want to talk to his girlfriend, Kelly Madigan. Instead he stayed glued to the all-news radio station, waiting to hear if someone had leaked the story of Diller Rourke's disappearance. But there wasn't a word.

On Saturday morning Pete woke up dying to know if he still had a case. Had Diller shown up for work yet? Or was this really a mystery? He had to find out.

He hopped into his Vega and drove fifty miles south

to Dalton Cemetery. When he got there it was an instant replay of the day before. Travis and the cast and crew of *The Suffocation II* were all on the scene. But there was nothing to do. They were all waiting for Diller.

"Good morning, kid," Marty Morningbaum said as he suddenly came jogging around a large family plot of tall gravestones. He was wearing white shorts and a white tennis shirt. "How's your dad?"

"Fine," Pete said automatically. "Have you heard from Diller Rourke yet, Mr. Morningbaum?"

"Not yet," he replied, looking unhappy.

"Well, are you going to call the police?"

Marty jogged in place and turned off his watch alarm, which was beeping. "What can I do, kid? I've seen this before. It's just another young actor deciding to flex his muscles, keep everyone waiting, and take some time off. It's a nuisance, but it isn't a federal case."

"So what are you going to do?"

"I'm going to do what every man, woman, and zombie on this film is doing. I'm going to wait until Diller thinks it's time to make his entrance. And I want you to do the same. No amateur investigating, kid. It's really not necessary."

Pete was silent for a moment, trying to decide whether this made sense. What would Jupe say? What about the fight in Diller's beach house? What about the broken glass? Put all that together with the weird stuff that went wrong on the first Suffocation picture and it sounded to Pete like a situation that needed investigating—now!

But before he could say anything, Marty Morningbaum's watch started beeping again. "Gotta go, kid," Marty said. "Catch you later."

Pete walked back to his car feeling a little confused. Was there a mystery to worry about or wasn't there? And why was he the only person in the world who thought that Diller's disappearance was suspicious? Well, Marty Morningbaum probably knew actors better than he did, Pete decided. Diller would probably show up on his own. In the meantime Pete was going to go out and buy a Jaguar! That part was too good to be true.

Quickly Pete drove down the road to the phone booth and called Jupe's cousin, Ty Cassey. Ty was a newcomer to Rocky Beach. And he was something different to everyone who knew him. To Pete, Ty was a guy who could make things work—especially cars.

To Bob, Ty was a question mark. Bob said he never knew when he could trust Ty.

But to Jupe, Ty was a complete surprise. One day he fell out of the sky and landed in Rocky Beach—boom! Suddenly Jupe had a long-lost, twenty-seven-year-old cousin from Long Island, New York, whom he had never even heard of. Now that Ty was in California, he spent half his time hanging around the junkyard, showing Pete how to fine-tune cars. The other half of the time he just plain hung around. No one knew where.

Ty answered the phone in his garage apartment on the seventh ring. Sometimes he didn't answer until the twelfth. The night before he hadn't answered at all. "S'up?" Ty asked.

"Ty, it's Pete. What do you say we go pick up a Jaguar today?"

"I don't know, Pete," Ty said, slurping his coffee in Pete's ear. "Their locks are easy but they're hard to hot-wire."

"Hey, I didn't mean steal one. I meant *buy* one."

Ty laughed. "Buy a Jag? Yeah, I could make time for that."

Before the morning was up, Pete and Ty had walked into the showroom of Exclusive Cars, Inc., of Hollywood, better known as Expensive Cars of Hollywood.

The name Marty Morningbaum opened a lot of doors in Hollywood. Two of those doors were on a dark green Jaguar XJ6, which Pete and Ty drove off the lot an hour later.

Once they were out of the car dealer's lot, they drove around Rocky Beach for hours. To break in the car, they said . . . and, of course, to make sure they were seen. And it gave Pete a chance to talk to someone about Diller Rourke, the broken glass, the crystal, and the strange warning Marble Ackbourne-Smith had given Pete.

"Why are you telling *me* and not your two buddies?" Ty asked.

"Because I want to handle things on my own for once, that's why," Pete said.

Ty nodded and smiled. "Go for it."

Eventually they drove to Pete's grease pit. It was in Titus Jones's junkyard, next to the trailer where The Three Investigators made their headquarters.

"We've got a day and a half to get this car into shape," Pete said, propping open the hood.

"It shouldn't be hard," Ty said, tapping the windshield-washer fluid tank with a screwdriver. "Let's get this baby out of here and put in a bigger tank."

They did that and added a small air pump to increase the pressure. Then, late in the afternoon, Pete ran home and borrowed some fake blood from his father for a test.

"Try it," Ty said to Pete, who was behind the wheel.

Pete hit the washer button and red blood squirted from the washer nozzles—but it sprayed in a tall arc that missed the windshield and landed on the roof of the car.

"Oh, brother," Pete said. "Jon Travis would tear our hearts out if he saw this mess." Suddenly Pete felt like he was suffocating again, like something was pressing down on his chest. He grabbed the steering wheel with both hands.

"What's wrong with you?" Ty asked.

"I don't know," Pete said, climbing out of the car to catch his breath. But secretly he did know. It was the jinx—the Suffocation jinx. Maybe that crystal had something to do with it. He reached into his jeans pocket and pulled out the pink stone. It felt hot in his hands again.

"What's that?" asked Ty.

"It's a crystal, undoubtedly rose quartz or pink tourmaline, highly polished. Because it has a point at only one end, it is called a single-terminated crystal."

Only one person could have said that. Pete looked around. There stood Jupiter Jones. Jupe, with rumpled black hair and a red T-shirt that said LOVE TOY, SOME ASSEMBLY REQUIRED. He was the shortest of the Three Investigators and the chunkiest. He was always on a diet and had recently taken up doing stretching exercises. His arms crossed, he stood next to Bob Andrews, taking in the whole scene. By the time he was finished looking around, Jupe would have a million questions and at least that many answers.

"The real question is not what is that, but why does Pete have it?" Jupiter said.

"Uh, someone gave it to me at, uh, the movie location," Pete said.

"It's a gift for Kelly, I'll bet," Bob said. He was wearing a button-down oxford shirt, chinos, and moccasins with no socks. Once the shy records keeper of The Three Investigators, Bob was now one of the most popular guys at school. Tall, blond, and good-looking, especially since he traded in his glasses for a pair of contacts, Bob was also the team's expert on girls.

"Yeah, Kelly," Pete said, remembering his girlfriend. He had purposefully "forgotten" to call her last night. And now he really had forgotten to call her this morning and afternoon. Knowing Kelly, Pete was in trouble up to his neck.

"Don't stand so close to the Jag, Bob," said Ty. "You're drooling on the chrome."

"I may go out and shoot my VW," Bob said. "Where'd you guys get this beautiful machine?"

"It's not ours. It belongs to Jon Travis, the horror movie director," Pete said.

"Too bad," Bob said, grinning at Pete. "Anyway, we're on our way down to the Ice Creamery to see who's hanging out. You guys want to come?"

"Can't," Pete said. But before Jupe and Bob left, he said, "Hey, Jupe. You know about actors. Do they sometimes just sort of not show up for work?"

"Sometimes?" Jupe laughed. "Frequently. And the bigger the star, the longer you wait."

"Can you think of something that's glass in a house that's not a window or a drinking glass or a mirror or a vase?"

Jupiter raised one eyebrow. Pete knew he wasn't thinking about Pete's questions. He was trying to figure out why Pete was asking it.

"What's going on?" Jupe asked.

"Nothing," Pete said, giving Ty a quick look. "It's not important. I'll tell you later."

When Jupe and Bob were gone, the two mechanics returned to wrestling with the car. But a few minutes later another distraction arrived. It was Pete's girl-friend, Kelly Madigan, a pretty brown-haired girl in blue jeans and a large-size man's dress shirt. She shook hands with Pete. "Hello. I'm Kelly Madigan. It's nice to meet you."

"What's the joke, babe?" asked Pete.

"Well," said Kelly, "since I haven't seen you or heard from you or received a letter, a note, or even a post card from you in two days, I thought you might have forgotten who I am."

Pete shook his head. "No, I recognized you the minute you drove up."

"Very funny, but you're missing the point," Kelly said. "I just saw Bob and Jupe on their way to the Ice Creamery. Why don't we go get a double malted? Big glass—two straws—lots of heavy eye contact."

"It sounds good, but I'm really busy, babe."

"Pete, there are probably hundreds of thousands of guys in this town who would like to go out with me," Kelly said. She stood with her hands on her hips and her head cocked to one side. Pete loved the way her hair fell across her face when she did that.

"Then why don't you go out with one of them?" Pete didn't know whether to get mad at Kelly or give in.

"Because I happen to be nuts about you, you walking lug wrench," Kelly said. "Hey, nice car." Her green eyes sparkled like the waxed finish of the Jaguar. "Can I take it for a spin?"

"We're working on it for a movie," Pete said.

"How about tomorrow morning?" Kelly asked.

"Well, I'm sort of working on a case," Pete said.

Kelly's impatience was turning to anger. "Don't kid me. When you're working on a case, it takes a crowbar to get you away from Jupe and Bob."

"I'm working on a case by myself. Is that so totally off the wall?"

"Is there anything in your life that isn't more important than I am?" Kelly snapped, getting back into her own car and slamming the driver's door. "Give me a call sometime. Maybe I'll be home."

Then she roared out of the junkyard.

Pete was frozen, but Ty started working again.

"What am I supposed to do?" Pete said. "She's totally unreal. Come on, Ty. You're twenty-seven. You ought to know how to handle stuff by now."

"Yeah, well, I can translate her message," Ty said. "She said, 'Call me tomorrow, or else.'"

Pete rubbed his hands on his jeans. He could feel the crystal in his right pocket. Suddenly he thought about Diller again and got that suffocating feeling.

"Let's finish this car fast," Pete said. "I've got to get back to the movie and start poking around."

They stayed up most of the night and by eight the next morning the car was ready. But it was Sunday, the film crew's day off. Pete tried calling Kelly all day, but she wasn't home. So he helped his dad with a new special effect and had to wait until after school on Monday to take the blood-gushing Jaguar to Jon Travis.

At the Hollywood movie studio where Travis was shooting, the guard at the gate let Pete drive right on through. All Pete had to do was squirt the bloody windshield washers once.

Pete found Travis inspecting sets being built on sound stage seven and digging a splinter out of his hand with a paper clip. As usual he wore black.

He's going to love the car when he sees it, Pete thought. But Travis wasn't paying attention.

"Mr. Travis," Pete began, "about your car—"

"Yeah, great," Jon Travis said with no enthusiasm at all. "Listen, I've got a meeting with Marty. Come on."

Pete followed along, just one of several people who

were trying to get ten seconds of Jon Travis's attention. They walked like a unit, glued together, across the studio lot to a two-story stucco office building. And then they walked into Marty Morningbaum's office, a large room filled with movie posters and photos of famous movie stars. The meeting had already started.

Marty was sitting on the edge of his huge walnut desk at one side of the room. Five people Pete didn't recognize, probably writers, and the different specialists—the director of photography, stunt coordinator, costume designer, and makeup artist—were there, too. They were scattered about on the low, overstuffed chairs and sofas that formed a semicircle around Morningbaum.

"Come in. Sit down. Good afternoon, kid. Hello, Jon," Marty said. His voice sounded tired.

Pete sat down in a low leather chair next to Jon Travis.

"I'll catch you guys up—but I haven't said anything we don't all know," Marty said. "It's time to face the fact that for whatever reason Diller is doing this, he may be gone for a while. So I am recommending we move back onto the lot for the castle sequences."

"It'll take my guys three days to finish the sets," said a woman with stiff black hair.

Pete slumped in his chair. Forget the car, he thought. Now Travis wouldn't use the Jaguar for weeks.

"We're virtually closed down anyway waiting for him to show," Jon Travis said angrily.

As Travis spoke, Marty Morningbaum's watch

beeped. A minute later an executive assistant brought in the afternoon mail. One piece, marked PERSONAL, hadn't been opened. Marty opened it idly while he listened to people talk. Suddenly in the middle of a discussion of burning flesh, Marty's face turned pale. "Oh, no," he moaned.

"What's wrong?" Jon Travis said. "Got a weak stomach, Marty? Can't take the blood and gore?"

"No," Morningbaum said. "It's Diller. He's been kidnapped!"

4

Halloween Horrors

THE RANSOM NOTE CRACKLED IN MARTY MORNING-baum's hand, the only sound in the room. Finally he laid it on his desk and nervously began to flatten it out. Everyone was speechless.

"What does the note say, Marty?" someone finally asked.

"It's a ransom note," Marty said numbly. "It says they want a lot of money or they'll kill the poor kid."

"How much money?" Jon Travis said.

"They don't say," Marty said. "See for yourself." He stood up and passed the note to a writer seated nearby. The note circulated around the room, but when it got to Jon Travis, he handed it back to Morningbaum instead of showing it to Pete. Then Morningbaum put it in a drawer in his desk.

Thanks a lot, Travis! Pete thought. I've got to get a look at that note! But the reality of the whole thing suddenly hit Pete in the stomach like a shovelful of wet earth. Diller was kidnapped. And Pete had unconsciously known it—or at least suspected—from the minute he walked into Diller's beach house.

Morningbaum picked up the envelope the ransom note had come in and pulled something else out.

"Oh, no!" he gasped. "There's a Polaroid." He dropped the photo on his desk.

People jumped out of their chairs and rushed to the desk to see the picture. But Pete only got a glimpse before Morningbaum put the Polaroid in the drawer with the ransom note.

Finally the woman with the stiff black hair reached for the telephone. "We've got to call the police," she said.

But Marty clamped his hand down on the phone fast. "No police. They'll kill Diller if I call the police. Do you think these animals are kidding around?"

No, they weren't kidding around. Pete was certain of that. And if they were smart, they'd move quickly and wrap this up fast while people were still feeling shocked and powerless.

"Mr. Morningbaum?" Pete spoke up. "Is there anything my friends and I can do? We *are* pretty good at this kind of thing—"

"Absolutely not!" Marty said. "Didn't you hear me say no police? No detectives, either! I mean it!"

"You know what this means, don't you, Marty," said Jon Travis.

"Yes. I've got to come up with a bundle of money to pay the ransom," Marty said.

"Yeah, yeah, that too," Travis said quickly. "But I'm talking about the film. We've got to shut down totally until this is over. And I'm not gonna be the one to tell the crew the bad news. Bad news is the producer's job."

Marty turned his tired eyes on Travis, and finally

nodded. "You're right, Jon. It's my job to tell them. Let's go to the set."

Great idea, thought Pete, eyeing Marty's desk again.

Marty left first, followed by the writers and the people who followed Jon Travis around. Pete went last, staying way behind them. When they were all out, he quickly stepped back into the office and closed the door. He rushed over and grabbed the ransom note from Marty's desk drawer.

The note was made from pasted-down words and letters cut out of a newspaper. It read: "We have Diller Rourke. It will cost you a lot of money to get him back. If you contact the police, you'll never see him alive again. Instructions to follow."

Then Pete looked at the Polaroid photo. It showed Diller sitting on a metal folding chair. His arms were stretched straight out behind him and tied to a wall, his mouth was covered with a wide band of white tape, his legs were bound at the ankles. His famous blue eyes stared wildly with the look of someone who could see his death standing in front of him.

Pete's stomach twisted at the photo, feeling the ropes biting into his own wrists and ankles, the tape sealing his own mouth. Stick to facts, not feelings, he told himself. That's what Jupe always says.

Pete high-geared it out of Marty's office with the ransom note hidden in his pocket and headed straight for the photocopier down the hall. He was glad he had noticed it on the way in. Good detective work, Pete, he congratulated himself.

He made several copies of the note and the horrible

photo, too. When he got back to Morningbaum's office, he breezed past the secretary saying, "I think I left something in there." Luckily she just nodded and didn't follow him in. Quickly Pete put the note back inside Morningbaum's desk.

Now what? This wasn't just a mystery anymore. It was a kidnapping case, a matter of life and death. And no matter how much he had wanted to handle it alone, he couldn't risk it when Diller's life was at stake. There was only one thing to do. Pete picked up the telephone and dialed a familiar number.

"Jupe? Pete. Don't go anywhere. Wait for me. I've got to talk to you and Bob. I can't talk now." He hung up just as the door opened.

Marty Morningbaum's secretary stared at Pete. "What are you doing?"

"Had to call my girl. Sorry," Pete said. He tossed the keys to the Jag on Marty's desk and walked quickly to the door.

Now with no car, Pete scrounged a lift back to Rocky Beach from a crew member. After a quick stop at home, he parked his car in the junkyard outside the Three Investigators' headquarters. He hopped out and bolted toward the trailer, but before he could open the door, Jupe called out to him from inside. "Hold it! You're wearing a green T-shirt, blue jeans, and your grubby basketball shoes. Right?"

"How'd you know that?" Pete asked.

Bob opened the door to the trailer. "Look up," he said.

Above Pete's head was a color video camera attached

to the trailer and turning from side to side, surveying
the area. It was Jupe's new security system, which he
had been working on for weeks. Inside, the monitor
sat in front of Jupe on his desk.

"Cool," Pete said as he stepped into the headquarters. "But listen, guys. I've got heavy news. Diller
Rourke's been kidnapped from his Malibu beach
house. I just happened to be there at a meeting this
afternoon when Marty Morningbaum—the producer
—got a ransom note."

"That was fast work, Pete. The trail is still hot," said
Jupe. "Let's hear the details."

Pete pushed the color monitor aside, sat down on
the desk, and rubbed his hands nervously on his jeans.
"Well . . . some of this you're not going to like. See,
I mean, the trail isn't too hot anymore, because,
well . . ."

"What?" Bob demanded. "Spit it out!"

"Because Diller was probably kidnapped three days
ago," Pete confessed.

"He was kidnapped three days ago, but you just
discovered that fact now?" Jupe asked.

"Huh-uh. I knew about it three days ago," Pete
said. In the silence Pete saw a small pout beginning to
form on Jupe's mouth. "I know what you're going to
say about the three of us sticking together and all that
stuff—and you're right. The truth is, at first I didn't
want you guys to help me. But now I do."

Jupe pouted for a minute more, but then he gave a
little shrug. "Oh, well, I guess I don't mind that you
did a little preliminary investigating."

"I'm glad you feel that way, Jupe," Pete said with a sly grin, "because I sort of told Mr. Morningbaum that I was the brains of this group, and I was calling in my assistants to help."

Bob burst out laughing.

"I will soon disabuse him of that erroneous perception," Jupe huffed.

"It was a joke, Jupe!" Bob said. "Clues you catch on to real fast. Jokes take longer."

Jupe's face flushed red. "Could I please see the ransom note?" he said, holding out his hand.

Pete showed them the photocopies of the ransom note and the hideous Polaroid.

"Whew," Bob said. "Ugly scene."

"If you're worried about Diller Rourke's physical well-being, I wouldn't be," Jupe said. "This photo was obviously staged to be as upsetting as possible. Notice that his arms are pinned back very far. If he remained like that for very long, he'd be unable to breathe and would probably faint. His abductors need to keep Diller in good shape for him to remain valuable."

"You know, there's something interesting about the ransom note," Bob said. "These words seem to be cut out of a newspaper. But it's not the L.A. *Times* or the *Herald-Examiner*. It's some other paper's headline type."

"What do you think? The note was sent from outside Los Angeles?" Pete asked.

"A very logical possibility, Pete," said Jupe. "Good thinking."

"Thanks," Pete said, beaming. "And there's a

bunch of other weird stuff you'd better hear about this case, too."

Pete started with the rumors about *The Suffocation* being a jinxed film and told them about Marble Ackbourne-Smith, his crystals, and his warning that Pete was in danger. "He saw it with his third eye. Then he said I should listen to the crystal," Pete said.

"If you start listening to crystals, you *are* in danger—of losing your mind!" Jupe said.

They talked until it got dark. Suddenly Pete said, "I need some food." So they left Headquarters and drove off in Pete's Vega. The night was crisp and there were witches and ghosts and skeletons everywhere.

"Hey, we forgot," Pete said. "Tonight's Halloween."

They cruised for a while, looking for kids from school. But mostly they just saw small groups of pint-sized trick-or-treaters. A few of them looked exactly like the blood-crazed zombies from *The Suffocation*.

After a pizza, when Pete braked at a stop sign, he turned on his windshield wipers. The wipers began to swing back and forth and then thick red blood squirted onto the windshield.

"What's that?" Jupe said, taken totally by surprise.

"Oh, no. I must have run over something juicy," Pete said with an innocent face.

"Unbelievable!" Bob said. "You rigged your car up like that stunt Jaguar, didn't you?"

Pete laughed. After that he only turned on the blood at traffic lights when they could gross out the maximum number of people.

Finally they drove back to Headquarters. Halfway

down the block Jupe pressed a remote-control button and an electronic door opener cranked open the main iron gates to the junkyard.

"Hey, look!" Bob said as soon as the car pulled up. "The trailer door has been kicked in!"

"That's not all," Jupe said with alarm. "The windows have been smashed!"

"Someone must have jumped the gate," Pete said angrily.

They piled out of Pete's car and ran into the trailer. The Three Investigators' files had been pulled open and dumped on the floor. The desk was covered with a thick blizzard of paper.

"I don't believe it. The place has been trashed!" Bob said.

Pete started feeling as if the walls were coming toward him. He let out a low moan.

"Pete—what's wrong?" Bob asked.

"It's the glass," Pete said. "We're stepping on glass, just like at Diller Rourke's house. I feel like I'm suffocating. I can't breathe."

Jupe walked over and pulled down sheets of newspaper that had been taped to the wall. He gasped when he read the message that was painted underneath. "Looks like you're right. This *is* about Diller Rourke," Jupe said in a shaky voice.

Pete and Bob looked up and read the message at the same time. It said:

Diller Rourke's blood is on your hands!

5

The Suffocation: Rated Zzzzz!

"**I** CAN'T BREATHE!" PETE REPEATED. HE GULPED FOR air. "I feel like I'm suffocating."

"It's your imagination," Jupe said, but he quickly opened the trailer door wider to let in more crisp October air. A couple of firecrackers suddenly exploded far away, down the street.

"It's going to take us years to clean up this mess," Bob moaned, looking around at the vandalized trailer.

"But more than that, someone's seen all of our secret files!" Jupe wailed. He pounded his meaty fists together.

"Calm down, Jupe," Bob said. Slowly he scanned the trailer with a puzzled look on his face. "Wait a minute. How did they even know we were working on this case?"

Jupe thought for a minute. "The kidnappers must have been keeping an eye on everyone connected with the film, including Pete," he said.

Pete helped Jupe lift an old metal file cabinet right-side up.

"Still, it's weird," Pete said. "The ransom note just came today, and I didn't even know I was being followed."

"Maybe we'll have a better idea of who we're up against after we look at our vandals," Jupe said.

"What are you going to do? Invite them to dinner?" Bob asked.

"In due time, perhaps," Jupe said. "But right now I'm going to see if my new video security system has done its job."

"Hey—that's right! The camera! You might have these guys on tape," Pete said.

"That's great," Bob said. "But how much tape do we have to watch before the vandals show up?"

"Give me a break," Jupe said as he rewound the tape. "Would I design a system with flaws? I've hidden an electric eye outside. When someone comes close to Headquarters, he or she trips the eye and that starts the video recorder. When they leave, the camcorder turns off."

Jupe pressed the play button and they watched the small color monitor. When the picture clicked on, the three friends leaned in close for a better look. But what they saw made them move back.

A tall, thin, eerie figure came out from the darkness to fill the screen. He seemed to sweep toward the trailer as if he were gliding, not walking. His long black cape puffed in the breeze.

Jupe suddenly hit the pause button so they could study his horrible, hypnotizing face.

It was fluorescent green, with smoldering red eyes like hot coals, and his cheeks were dark, deep hollows. He looked as if he were in pain—a pain that burned from the inside out.

"Wow," Pete said in a low voice.

Jupe started the tape again. The eerie figure looked behind him and all around him, once, twice. Then, confident that no one was watching, he raised his foot and gave the door to the trailer a solid kick. The door banged open and the intruder entered Headquarters, disappearing from the camera's view. In a few minutes he left, his cape flowing behind him as he quickly walked away.

"Who is he?" asked Bob.

"What is he?" asked Pete.

They watched the videotape again and again, each time noticing something else about the intruder.

"He's got fangs," Bob said.

"He's wearing a ring with a large jewel on his right hand," Jupe said.

When they had memorized every move the figure made and every ghoulish detail about him, they turned off the machine.

"You gotta admit it's the perfect crime," Pete said. "Dress up in a vampire costume on Halloween so no one can recognize you. In a disguise like that you could get away with murder." The word hit them like fake blood shot from a splatter gun.

"All right. It's time for a plan," Jupe said. "Pete, tomorrow you'll take us to the studio. We need to establish some suspects by talking to the people who knew Diller best—and saw him *last*."

But when they got to the studio the next day after school, the first person they ran into was Pete's dad.

He was walking across the studio lot carrying an exploding face mask.

"Hey, guys. You're just in time," said Mr. Crenshaw. "I'm going over to look at the dailies to see how my effects are coming out. Want to take a look?"

As they followed Mr. Crenshaw to a private screening room on the studio lot Bob asked, "What are dailies?"

"That's what they call all the film that was shot each day," Pete said, feeling proud to be an expert on something Bob didn't know. "It's all the unedited takes, full of mistakes and everything."

The screening room was like a miniature theater with six rows of red plush velvet movie seats. Each seat in the front row had an intercom button on the arm. Pete's dad sat down, hit the talk button, and asked the projectionist to play the film.

The lights dimmed and the film began to roll.

The Three Investigators watched all the special effects scenes shot in the past week. Ordinary everyday situations—but every one of them had a bloody Jon Travis twist to it.

In one scene a little kid had a bad case of hiccups.

"I know how to fix those," said the boy's mother, who had turned into a zombie. "I'll *scare* you."

Then, without saying another word, she ripped off the boy's arm. Blood squirted from his shoulder as he screamed in pain.

"See. No more hiccups," she said.

"Cut!" yelled Jon Travis from offscreen. "How can you top perfection?"

In another scene a man sneezed, then stared in

horror into his handkerchief, which was filled with his own brains!

Jupe leaned over to Bob and whispered, "Jon Travis is an intense personality."

"Takes one to know one," Bob whispered back.

Then they watched Diller Rourke in some of his scenes. When he turned into a zombie, dark circles of makeup under his eyes produced the desired effect.

"I know you wanted me to go to Harvard, Dad," Diller the zombie said on the screen. "But I'm happier biting peoples' faces off."

"Who wrote this script?" Pete whispered loudly. "Lassie?"

"Ouch," said Pete's dad. "Take it easy, guys. This is my job you're talking about."

A new scene came on, with Diller and a beautiful young actress. She was short, with curly dark hair and even curlier eyelashes. Exactly Jupe's type.

"Isn't that Victoria Jansen?" asked Jupe, leaning forward.

"Right," said Mr. Crenshaw. "She's sort of the co-star of the film, although her face explodes in the first twenty minutes. She and Diller used to date each other. In this scene she's baby-sitting and doesn't know that Diller has just eaten the two little kids upstairs in their bedrooms."

"You've got to believe me, Kathy," Diller was saying on the screen to Victoria, "I get these weird feelings. It's like I can't breathe. I feel like I'm in a grave and all these guys are shoveling heavy dirt on top of me. It makes me want to kill somebody."

"Oh, Diller," said the actress in Diller Rourke's arms. "It's only your imagination. You wouldn't hurt a fly."

"Cut!" yelled Jon Travis offscreen. "Victoria, you called him Diller!"

"I'll bet they release this movie during Thanksgiving," Bob commented.

"Why?" Pete asked.

"Because that's when everyone wants some turkey!"

Pete and Jupe cracked up and started making gobbling noises and hooting.

"Come on, guys. Is it really that bad?" asked Mr. Crenshaw.

Pete and Bob waited for Jupe to comment. He had been a movie star when he was a tiny kid and always had strong opinions about films—along with everything else, of course.

"The script is ridiculous and the director is totally out of control," Jupe said. "This is what always happens when a low-budget director like Jon Travis has one big hit. The studio triples the budget for his next film, gives him total artistic control, and the guy becomes a total egomaniac. *Mondo Grosso* went to Travis's head. You wanted to hear the truth, didn't you, Mr. Crenshaw?"

"Give me a minute to think about that, Jupiter," said Pete's dad with a strained smile.

When they'd seen all the dailies, Pete, Jupe, and Bob got up to start roaming the studio, sniffing for clues about Diller Rourke. But Pete's dad stopped them.

"Marty Morningbaum called me in this morning,

Pete," Mr. Crenshaw said. "He's afraid you guys will jeopardize Diller's safety with an amateur investigation."

"Dad—"

"I know," Mr. Crenshaw said. "You guys are good. But Marty's decided to go along with the kidnappers. And he told me to be sure you don't interfere. So—sorry, but I want you to leave."

No amount of protesting was going to change the truth—and the truth was that Pete had to do what his dad asked. So the Three Investigators grudgingly piled back into Pete's car and drove into the glittery lights of L.A. at sundown.

With Pete at the wheel and Bob next to him in charge of the radio, Jupe sat in the back seat talking about what Jon Travis was doing wrong.

"He's obviously jealous of Diller Rourke's scene with Victoria Jansen."

"He is or you are?" asked Bob.

"He's photographing her with terrible lighting and the angles are completely wrong," Jupe insisted.

They were stopped at a light. Bob flipped the radio dial, looking for bands he might know from his job at the talent agency. Suddenly Pete ripped open his seat belt and ran out of the car, leaving the door open. They were across from a Tex-Mex Burger Bar-B-Q Pit. Cars behind them started honking.

"Are you berserk?" Jupe yelled as Pete sprinted across the street toward the restaurant.

"It's Kelly! With another guy!" Pete shouted back. He darted across the road, spun away from pedestrians, and hurdled the row of cactuses that bordered the restaurant. Pete's target was a shiny black late-model Escort EXP parked in the Tex-Mex lot. A girl was getting in on the passenger side.

He got there just as a guy, a tall guy with dark hair cut in a flattop, pulled open the driver's door. Even though the guy looked like a body builder, Pete grabbed him by the T-shirt and pushed him away. Then Pete dipped his head through the door. "What's the big idea, Kelly?" he said.

"What's the big idea yourself?" asked the girl sitting in the passenger seat.

It wasn't Kelly.

Pete felt like a jerk . . . a complete jerk. Then he felt hands grabbing his shoulders from behind and spinning him around. "What's your problem, mold-face?" the guy snarled.

Pete had only a second to decide what to do next. Tell this guy it was a mistake or try to drop him with a couple of his patented lightning karate chops? Before he could choose, the big guy slipped in a quick hard one to Pete's stomach that knocked the wind out of him.

"Hey, it was a mistake!" Pete said, breathing hard. "I thought your girl was my girl."

"Can't you keep track of your girlfriends?" asked the other guy.

"We had a fight. A big one," Pete explained.

"Well, she's not in my car, Jack. So look somewhere else."

"Yeah," Pete said, watching the guy climb into his black car and speed away.

I'd better call Kelly, Pete thought to himself, before she gets *really* mad. But before he could find a phone, Jupe and Bob came up to him.

"Boy, you've got a strange way of making new friends," Bob said.

"Ha, ha. Let's just get something to eat. I'm hungry," Pete said as they walked back toward his car.

"We can go to my house," Bob said. "My mom's out tonight."

Half an hour later the Three Investigators were mounting a full-scale attack on Bob's kitchen. Jupe stuck the copy of the ransom note on the refrigerator with a small magnet so they could look at it and keep talking about the case while they ate. Then Jupe sat down in front of a tall cheese and sprouts on pumpernickel sandwich, just staring at it.

"Aren't you going to eat, Jupe?" Bob asked.

"Mental discipline," Jupe said. "That's part of my new diet. My body will eat when *I* say it can. To prove that I'm in control, I always wait fifteen minutes."

"Yeah—then you clean your plate like a vacuum cleaner!" Pete said.

Jupe ignored Pete's joke and stared hard at the sandwich. "Laugh if you want. I'm showing this sandwich who's the boss around here!"

"Has this been scientifically tested?" Bob asked Pete. "I mean, if he totally dominates that food, will the calorie count go down?"

"Oh, shut up," Jupe tried to say through a mouthful of bread, sprouts, and cheese.

Bob turned his attention to the ransom note stuck on the fridge door. " 'Instructions to follow,' " he read. "Do you think Marty Morningbaum has gotten his instructions yet?"

Just then Bob's father came into the kitchen. "Excuse me, guys. I've got to get a cup of coffee," he said. Mr. Andrews opened the refrigerator for some low-fat milk. "What's this?" he asked, nodding toward the ransom note.

"We're working on a case, Dad," Bob said.

Mr. Andrews had worked for a Los Angeles newspaper for years. He studied the ransom note while he sipped his coffee. "Hey, Bob. These words were all cut out of *Daily Variety*. Did you know that?"

"*Daily Variety?* That's the show-business trade newspaper," Pete said.

"Are you certain, Mr. Andrews?" Jupe asked.

"Jupiter, I know newspapers the way you know diets," Bob's father said as he left the kitchen.

Jupe pinched his lower lip, deep in thought.

"You know what this means, don't you?" Jupe's voice grew unusually quiet. "It means that whoever kidnapped Diller Rourke is probably involved in the movie business. Maybe even in *The Suffocation II!*"

6

The Young and the Restless

EVERYONE IN THE KITCHEN WAS SILENT FOR A minute. They just stared at the ransom note.

"Someone on the crew kidnapped Diller Rourke?" Bob said, repeating Jupe's conclusion.

"Or an actor, maybe," Jupe said. "I'm sure of it. Ordinary criminals don't read *Variety*. But everyone in show business does. It's practically Hollywood's bible. Yes, with this clue I think we've got this case practically solved."

Pete and Bob knew that was Jupiter Jones talk for "We've got our first strong lead."

"All we need is a suspect, a motive, and the location where Diller Rourke is being held," Pete said.

"Details, details," said Jupe. "All we really need is to focus this investigation logically. That is, question the cast and crew of *The Suffocation II* and sift out Diller's friends from his enemies. And as for a plan, I'm in favor of starting with Victoria Jansen, the actress we saw in the dailies."

"I'll bet you are," Bob said.

"After all, she was filming with Diller the day before he disappeared," Jupe said. "And Pete's father said they used to be romantically involved."

"*Used* to be? Hey, that means there's still a chance for you, Jupe," Pete said with a grin.

"Yeah, maybe she likes the weak, talkative type," Bob teased.

"You mean the robust, articulate type," Jupe corrected. "Hey—I'm ready."

"Anyway, Jupe, I've got bad news for you. Victoria Jansen is not going to be easy to talk to," Pete said. "My dad says she's super private and a real nut about disguise. She makes a game about no one recognizing her in public."

"A nut about disguise . . ." Jupe said. "I wonder where she was on Halloween?"

◆　　◆　　◆

It wasn't until the next afternoon that Pete's faded orange Vega roared into The Jones Salvage Yard, its horn beeping. "Jupe! Let's go! I found her."

Jupe came out of his electronics workshop, a shed next to their trailer headquarters. "What's going on?"

"Come on. Get in. My dad just told me some hot news," Pete said, speeding off. "Victoria Jansen is hanging out at a retirement home in Anaheim, doing research for her next movie."

"Victoria Jansen? Stop the car!" Jupe shouted. Pete braked and Jupe jumped out. He ran into his house across the street, returning ten minutes later in a clean pair of jeans and an ironed oxford dress shirt. "Now I'm ready," he said. "Where's Bob?"

"Couldn't come." Pete and Jupe said it together.

"Sax Sendler needed him to work at the music agency—as usual," Pete explained.

Jupe groaned. "Sometimes I think we should call ourselves the Two and a Half Investigators."

After more than an hour of hard driving, Pete pulled into the parking lot of a three-building retirement complex.

"Sylvan Woods Rest Home," Jupe read. "Talk about false advertising. It's not sylvan, and there are no woods anywhere—just a freeway."

"Well, it won't be hard to find Victoria Jansen here," Pete said, looking around at all of the white-haired people.

"Yes, I know," said Jupiter. "She'd stand out in any crowd, but especially this one."

They walked around the facilities, checking the game room, the TV room, the card room. The elderly residents were sitting in chairs or strolling around the grounds with their canes and walkers. They were talking, crocheting, gardening, and reading. Everyone seemed to notice the two teenagers but at first no one spoke to them.

"Hey, sonny."

Jupe and Pete turned toward a bench that was shaded by a large palm tree. An old woman, her gray hair drooping and unpinned under a large straw hat, was motioning to them with a crooked finger. She sat on the bench with a light blanket over her lap, covering her legs.

Pete and Jupe walked over to her and she patted the bench for them to sit down. Her smile creased her wrinkled skin even more. "My name's Maggie. You look lost."

"We're looking for a woman," Jupe said.

"What am I? Chopped liver?" said Maggie. The old woman accompanied her remark with a quick bat of her eyelashes.

Jupe smiled. "We're looking for someone younger," he said.

"You mean like Rosie? She's sixty-eight," Maggie said.

"We're looking for a young woman, an actress," Jupe explained.

"You fellas reporters or something?"

"No, we're detectives," Pete said.

"Oh, detectives? Got a heater? Got a rod? Got a gat?" said Maggie, using all the old-fashioned words for gun.

"No, we're not TV detectives," Pete said.

"We need to ask her some questions about someone who needs our help," Jupe said, looking around. Then he looked straight at Maggie. "You will help us, won't you, Miss Jansen?" he asked.

Maggie pushed her hat back on her head and her gray wig came off with it. Victoria Jansen's dark curls came bubbling out from under it. She was a strange sight, with her old face and young, vibrant hair. "How did you know?" she asked, her voice suddenly sounding much younger.

"The dialogue. 'Got a heater? Got a rod? Got a gat?' " Jupe said. "You said that in *The French Agent*, which I happened to rent two weeks ago."

"You keep your eyes and ears open, don't you?" Now that the actress was speaking as herself, she seemed nervous. She sat up straight, losing the bent-over posture of an old woman. She took off the lap robe, revealing her slender legs in tight blue jeans.

"In my next film I'm playing a character named Maggie who ages from twenty to eighty. I realized that I don't know the first thing about being eighty. So I came over here to watch. A good actor has to be a good observer." She looked directly at Jupe. "Ever think of being an actor?"

"Are you kidding?" Pete said. "Jupe used to be—"

But the rest of Pete's sentence, "Baby Fatso in the movies," was drowned out by Jupiter clearing his throat as loudly as he could.

"We want to talk to you about Diller Rourke," Jupe said.

The actress shook her head. "That's personal, guys."

"We're not looking for gossip," Jupe said. "We need information. When was the last time you saw him? What did you talk about? Did he say anything about anyone threatening him? We don't care about your romantic involvement with him."

"Well, I care," she answered. She squirmed on the bench and played with a ring on her right hand. "We had something going for about a year and then he just dropped me. It made a loud noise and it hurt. I was such a mess I even turned down work."

"Are you saying that you wouldn't mind if he were in serious trouble?" Jupe asked.

"I didn't say that. He's a guy who likes to take walks. He took one from me. He took one from the movie," Victoria said. She looked over at Pete. "You don't say much."

"I know what it's like to be dumped, too," Pete said, thinking of Kelly. He'd been trying to reach her for days. "But I was at Diller's house last Friday morning. I know he's in trouble."

After a moment, Victoria said, "I was there the night before."

"You were?" asked Jupe.

"We had dinner at his house, for old time's sake," she said. "I'd finished my work on *The Suffocation* that day. What was I? The last person to see him before he took off or something?"

"No," Jupe said. "The kidnappers saw him last."

"Kidnappers?" The word gave Victoria a chill. "Does Marty know?"

"He got the ransom note," Pete answered.

"Poor Marty. It must be killing him."

"Can you tell us about your evening with Diller?"

"We had a nice dinner. He was even making jokes about being an idiot for dumping me. He was okay that night."

"Could you tell us who Diller's friends and enemies are?" Jupe asked.

"I could give you a suspect list a mile long," said Victoria. "Try Richard Faber. He was supposed to get the starring role in *The Suffocation II* until suddenly Diller got it. Or maybe that New Age guru of his had something to do with the kidnapping. Diller always does what Marble Ackbourne-Smith tells him to do."

"You've been very helpful," Jupe said.

"I hope I don't regret it," the actress said, adjusting her hat and her wig and returning to her craggy

Maggie voice. "Well, boys, sure you don't want to stick around? We're all going to try on each other's false teeth later."

Pete and Jupe laughed and said good-bye to Victoria. As they climbed back into Pete's car Jupe said, "First thing tomorrow after school, we go back to the movie studio—no matter what your dad says."

"No way," said Pete. "I've got to try to make up with Kelly tomorrow. I haven't seen her for days."

"Kelly can wait," Jupe said. "Marty Morningbaum may have heard from the kidnappers by then. And you can talk to him and keep him busy."

"Keep him busy? For what?"

"Let's just say I'm going to take a tour of the studio— an unofficial tour of the studio," was Jupe's reply.

Keep Marty Morningbaum busy. Right, Pete thought. And he thought it again the next day as he sat outside Marty's office.

But how was he supposed to do it? With fast talk and sneaky tricks? That was Bob and Jupe's department. Well, too bad. If they could do it, Pete could at least try. Hey, Marty, how about those Rams? And have you heard the joke about . . .

Fortunately for Pete, however, Marty Morningbaum wasn't even there. He was keeping himself busy. Pete glanced around the reception room. The guy sitting on the chair across from Pete was waiting for Morningbaum too. He had thick dark hair that was slicked back, and he was wearing sunglasses with bright blue frames. He tapped his fingers, he tapped his feet. High-energy guy. Not very tall, but strong.

Occasionally he did push-ups on Marty's thick rug.

"Bench press two-ten," he told Pete.

"Two-twenty," Pete said.

The guy cleared away a wooden coffee table and squatted on his knees, resting his right elbow on the table, open palm in the air.

"Arm wrestling in a movie producer's office?"

"Why not?" asked the guy.

Pete got down on his knees and set his right arm. He locked palms and fingers with the guy and stared into his eyes.

"Go!" the guy said.

The table shook as each tried to force the other's hand down. Pete held on, saving his strength. He's got power, he thought, but not stamina.

Then the other guy blinked.

He's getting tired. Now! Pete thought. He gave it everything he had, driving his opponent's hand to the table top. The guy cried out—not in pain but in defeat.

Just then Marty Morningbaum walked into his outer office. He looked confused at finding two people on their knees in his reception room.

Pete's opponent jumped to his feet and latched onto Morningbaum. "How long are you going to wait, Marty?" he said.

"Richard, will you calm yourself," said Marty Morningbaum in his patient voice. "Is yelling at me going to make you happy?"

"You want to make me happy, Marty? Make up your mind," said the young man. "I was supposed to have the lead in *The Suffocation II* in the first place.

And the rumors are flying that Diller's taken a walk. You want to salvage this film? Shoot new principal camera work with *me* in the lead."

This guy didn't have to introduce himself now. Pete knew it was Richard Faber, the actor Victoria Jansen had told them about.

"Richard, it's out of my hands. You don't know. We'll talk soon," Marty said.

Richard glared at Pete. "Who's this? The next guy who's going to steal a role from me?" The fiery actor pushed past Pete to leave.

Marty gave Pete a tired look. His face was gray. "How are you, kid? We were very pleased with your car. Did you want to speak to me?"

Pete took a deep breath and followed Marty into his large office. On Marty's desk was another piece of Pete's father's work—an eyeball with a fork in it. This movie *is* a turkey, Pete thought. He's got every dumb gag you can think of. "Mr. Morningbaum, I've been wondering about Diller. Have the kidnappers made contact with you?"

The producer shook his head. Then he picked up The Three Investigators' business card that Pete had given him. "I can trust you to stick to our plan of not getting involved, can't I, kid? I want everyone to do everything the kidnappers ask, so that nothing will happen to Diller."

Pete nodded. Convincingly, he hoped. "It's just strange. Usually they make contact fast. Take the money and run. I can't figure what they're waiting for."

"Do you know a lot about kidnappers, kid?" Marty asked with something like a smile.

"We've solved a kidnapping case or two," Pete said proudly. "I know you want me to back off," he added, "but I brought my friend Jupiter to the studio today. I thought maybe we could check into some of Diller's friends. They might know something."

Marty Morningbaum thought hard for a minute, staring off into space.

"Good idea, kid. I'll tell you who to start with. Marble Ackbourne-Smith. There's definitely something flake-o about that guy."

The crystal, which Pete had been carrying in his pocket, suddenly seemed to get hot again.

"Thanks for the tip," Pete said as he hurried to find Jupe. By now Jupiter would have questioned three dozen people and probably discovered what Diller Rourke's favorite food was when he was twelve. But wait till Jupe heard about Pete's meeting with Richard Faber. The suspects were mounting up.

Pete looked all over the studio for almost an hour and couldn't find Jupe. He wasn't on the sound stage and he wasn't in the cafeteria. Where *was* he?

Suddenly Pete turned a corner in a scenery shop and almost tripped over something that some jerk had left in the middle of the floor.

"Oh, no!" Pete cried out.

He couldn't believe his eyes. There on the floor was Jupiter Jones . . . flat on his back . . . with a big bloody gash across his throat!

7

Marble Jumps In

"NO!" PETE SHOUTED. FOR A MOMENT HE DIDN'T know whether to run for help or just stay there in case Jupe came to for a few last minutes on earth. Pete's cry roared and rumbled and died in the empty scenery shop.

He dropped to his knees, next to the lumplike body of his good friend. Anger and pain filled his chest, but when he tried to talk he had to fight back a sob. "Jupe, who did this to you?" Pete cried out. He slammed his hand on the concrete floor. "You gotta tell me, Jupe. You gotta tell me what to do now! I count on you to have the plans, Jupe."

Pete jumped up, his heart pounding with fear. Where could he find help? The gash in Jupe's throat was too horrible to contemplate. The body didn't move. He had to be dead . . .

Pete started breathing hard again, feeling the walls pressing in and the ceiling pressing down on him. "Jupe, you gotta tell me . . . you gotta tell me . . . you gotta tell me—why you aren't bleeding?" Pete suddenly finished, looking at the floor beside Jupe. He touched it. The floor was dry and dusty, not wet and bloody. Then he reached out his hand toward the deep red slash across Jupe's neck.

It was rubber.

"Movie makeup," Pete snarled, giving Jupe a shove. "Okay, joker, the gag's over. And it wasn't funny!"

But Jupe still didn't move— not even after Pete gave him a good hard shake. This wasn't a joke. Something *was* wrong with Jupe. Pete quickly felt his friend's neck for a pulse. "He's not dead, but he sure is out." What was going on around here?

Slowly Jupe's head began to roll on his neck as if it needed tightening. A low moan came from his dry lips. Finally he opened his eyes.

"Welcome back," Pete said with a smile. "Don't forget to stop at baggage claim and pick up your head."

Jupe stared at Pete without moving or speaking.

"Can't you talk?"

"Shh," scolded Jupiter. "I'm reconstructing every-thing that happened."

"Do it out loud."

Jupe sat up, weaving unsteadily. "Let's see . . ." he began. "I was nosing around where Jon Travis was setting up to film some interior scenes for the movie. And I was talking with crew members. They gave me some crucial information."

"About Diller?"

"Well, no. About dieting, as a matter of fact," Jupe said with a small grin.

"*Jupe!*"

"Protein milk shakes, Pete. That's what all the stars use to maintain their weight. And they said it really works. So naturally I went directly over to the studio commissary to get one. While I was waiting for my drink, I noticed a very large man watching every move I made. Of course, I acted as if I hadn't noticed him. But as I left with my milk shake he blocked the doorway.

"For a moment we looked at each other. And then he said, 'In life, what's important is not what we find but that we have something to look for.' "

"Oh, no. I don't believe it," Pete said, smacking his forehead with his hand. "That had to be Marble Ackbourne-Smith."

"It was indeed," said Jupiter. He stood up and took a few shaky steps. Pete reached out, ready to catch him if he fell.

"I'm all right," Jupe said. "Let me go on. I couldn't leave the commissary with my milk shake because this Marble person wanted to give me the answers to everything—everything except the questions I asked him. Finally I asked him when was the last time he saw Diller Rourke. 'I see him every day,' he said."

"You're kidding. Where?"

" 'My third eye can see him,' he told me. Third eye? He doesn't know how to use the two he's got. Then I said to him, 'Where is Diller Rourke?' He was just about to tell me when Marty Morningbaum came up to us. He recognized me, of all things—as Baby Fatso! He said they were trying out some new horror makeup and would I like to let them try it on me."

Jupe pulled the gory rubber slice off his neck. He had to pull hard to loosen the rubber cement. "As you can see, I agreed to be their guinea pig since I thought it would give me an opportunity to speak with Morningbaum further. But I was wrong. He took me to the makeup department and left me. A while later he came back to inspect the job. But before I could ask him anything, his watch beeped and he ran out."

"What did you do then?" asked Pete.

"I went back to the commissary, where I had left Marble and my milk shake. Marble was gone but my milk shake was there. I drank the rest as I walked back here. I don't remember what happened after that— until I saw you."

"The milk shake was drugged, Jupe. It had to be. And I'll bet Marble did it." Pete looked around.

"If you're looking for the milk shake cup—forget it. It was right there on the bench, and it's gone," Jupe said. "So I think we'd better talk to Marble Ackbourne-Smith. The sooner the better."

Marble Ackbourne-Smith was not difficult to find. He had an ad in the Los Angeles yellow pages under Spiritual Consultants. It read: "Marble Ackbourne-Smith, seer, prognosticator, healer, channeler, notary public. The world is my answering machine. It leaves messages for me and I return its calls."

The address in the ad led Pete and Jupe to a large, long white ranch house in Beverly Hills. The front door was standing wide open, even though the house was filled with expensive furniture and paintings. Pete and Jupe knocked. When no one answered, they walked in and went through the house to the back. There, by a diamond-shaped swimming pool, Marble sat in the warm evening air. He was bare chested, wearing loose long white linen pants, with his legs folded in the lotus position. The moon was rising and a single evening star twinkled in the sky like the lights in the pool.

"Jupe, I know this guy from somewhere," Pete whispered.

"Of course. You saw him several days ago. He gave you a pink tourmaline," answered Jupe impatiently.

"No. From somewhere else," Pete said.

Jupe shrugged and approached the muscular blond cross-legged man by the pool.

There were four large blue crystals around Marble, making a perfect square. He held a red stone in his hand. There were small white crystals tucked inside his ears and a gold rock in his navel. His eyes were closed.

"Mr. Ackbourne-Smith, I want to continue the conversation we were having," Jupe said, trying to get Marble's attention.

Without opening his eyes, Marble said, "I can't hear you. I have a crystal in my ear."

"New age. Old jokes," muttered Jupe.

"The crystals in my ears block out negative vibrations that jar our deeper understanding of who we could become if only we were someone else," Marble said. "They also tell me that a poison has invaded your body."

"I doubt if you needed a crystal to tell you that, since I suspect you are the person who poisoned me," Jupe said. "What exactly did you put in my protein milk shake?"

Marble laughed, stood up, and rearranged the

crystals on the ground by the swimming pool. "It's almost six o'clock," he said. "Time for my daily swim." With that, he made a running leap into the deep end of his diamond-shaped pool.

Pete and Jupe watched Marble thrash about wildly as his head bobbed in and out of the water. His eyes grew large and his mouth filled with water.

"He's not much of a swimmer," said Jupe.

"Jupe, he can't swim a stroke!" Pete suddenly realized. He yanked off his shoes and dived into the water after Marble. In clean, strong strokes he reached the drowning man in seconds. He wrapped his arm around Marble's neck from behind and towed the large man to the side.

It took all of Pete's and Jupe's strength to haul Marble out of the pool.

When Marble was finally out, Jupe said, "Why did you do that? You could have drowned if we hadn't been here."

"You weren't here yesterday," Marble said. "I swam then."

"We're not going to be here in another minute, either," Jupiter said in frustration. Pete took one look at his friend and knew that Marble had really pushed Jupe's tension button. "I'm going to be very direct with you," Jupe went on. "Diller Rourke has been kidnapped. I suspect you know something about it that you are not telling us. That's your decision. But don't think for a moment that it will stop us from finding out everything we need to know about you."

Pete saw that Jupe's words pushed a few of Marble's

tension buttons too. For an instant a tight-lipped glare pushed aside the guru's contented smile. But Marble centered himself again just as quickly.

"I cannot tell you where Diller is," he said. "But Diller can tell me where he is."

"Are you expecting him to call?" asked Jupe.

"Diller is a student of mine," Marble explained. "The first thing I do is give my students their own crystals. Our crystals become tuned to us. They know us. They know our thoughts, our dreams. They help us pick out our clothes. And when we are miles away, they are lonely for us."

"In twenty-five words or less, what are you trying to say?" Jupe demanded, ready to explode.

"Bring me Diller's crystals and I will tune them and program them and channel with them," Marble said.

"Sounds like cable TV," muttered Pete.

Marble closed his eyes. "Bring me the crystals. They will tell me where Diller is."

"Crystals are going to tell you where Diller Rourke is? Right." Pete drew out the last word as he shook his head in disbelief. "What if the crystals don't know? What if they're having a bad day and don't feel like telling you?"

"Crystals are the universal lost and found," Marble said.

This guy's so full of baloney he'd qualify for cafeteria food, Pete thought.

But to Pete's surprise, Jupe said, "Okay, it's a deal. We'll find the crystals and bring them to you as fast as we can."

8

Crystal Unclear

PETE GRUMBLED ALL THE WAY TO HIS CAR. "I'M telling you, Jupe, I know this guy from somewhere. I just can't remember from where. And how come you agreed to look for the crystals? Usually you steamroller a guy like that, with all of the philosophy books you've read."

Jupe smiled as he got into Pete's car and buckled the seat belt. "You're right, but I couldn't do that this time. There is something that Marble Ackbourne-Smith wants to tell us. Or something he's hiding— I'm not sure which. Either way, we have to play along with him if we want to learn more. Besides, if we do find Diller's crystals, we may also find a clue."

The first logical place to look for the crystals was Diller Rourke's Malibu beach house. Pete drove and Jupe talked on and on about his theories regarding Marble, Jon Travis, Richard Faber, and even Victoria Jansen.

After about an hour, Pete turned unexpectedly into a Chicken Coop restaurant.

"Are you hungry?" Jupe asked.

"No, I just want to watch you stare down some fried

chicken," Pete said. "At least you'll be quiet for fifteen minutes."

After the pit stop, Pete drove straight to Diller's house. But when they got out of the car, Pete was reluctant to go in. He approached the front door cautiously. It was still unlocked.

Pete peered inside. Nobody had righted the furniture or the odd four-footed sculpture.

"The place hasn't been touched," Pete said.

"Lead the way," ordered Jupe.

So Pete stepped in. *Crunch, crunch*. The shards of broken glass were now mixed with a fine layer of sand, which the wind had blown up from the beach.

"A prime-time fight must have gone on here," Pete said.

"I see what you mean," said Jupe, surveying the topsy-turvy room. He squatted down and examined the floor. "This glass is not from crystals. The pieces are uneven. A crystal, when it breaks, shatters into smaller crystals."

"So where'd it come from?"

"It's a mystery," Jupe said ruefully.

When they began to search the house for Diller's crystals, Pete set to work in the living room. A while later Jupe called loudly from the back of the house.

"Look at this!"

Pete dashed down the hall and into the back bedroom, which faced the ocean. There he found Jupiter Jones squatting by a bookshelf, looking at a book.

"Autographed copies of Marble Ackbourne-Smith's

books," Jupe said, and then began to read their titles aloud. "*Infinity Stops Here. Out-of-Body Experiences, or How to Be Your Own Best Travel Agent. The Third Eye Book of Optical Illusions. Getting Rich by Going Broke: An Autobiography.*"

Pete suddenly felt as though he couldn't breathe. "The crystals aren't here, Jupe. I'm going back to the car. Let's look somewhere else."

Thirty minutes passed before Jupe joined Pete in his car outside of Diller's house.

"What took you so long?" Pete asked.

"I used the phone to call Victoria Jansen," Jupe explained. "She said that Diller never filmed a single day without his crystals. He used his topaz when he was doing a horror scene, his amethyst when he was doing a romantic scene, and his quartz when he was filming the 'buried alive' scene, which they were supposed to shoot the day he disappeared. She said they did close-ups of Diller in his casket the day before."

"So where are we going?" Pete asked. "To the movie studio?"

"To the cemetery," Jupe said.

"Cemetery! Jupe, why do our cases always end up in a cemetery? I've spent so much of my life in cemeteries, I ought to have my mail sent there! Can't we do something different for a change and go there during the day?"

"You mean instead of the *dead* of night?" Jupe asked with a smile. "It is very possible that Diller Rourke left his crystals in the casket that was used during the filming last Thursday. And according to Victoria Jansen, the props and the film trucks are still at the cemetery."

"But come on, Jupe. Not tonight. It's more than fifty miles away. I bet it'll even be midnight by the time we get there."

Pete was wrong. It was exactly 11:59 P.M. when they killed the headlights across the street from Dalton Cemetery. A dry November wind whipped through the trees. It made the branches bend and sway as though they were having a conversation with each other.

"Maybe I should stay here and keep the motor running and the radio playing," Pete said.

Jupe handed Pete a flashlight from the glove compartment. "Don't worry. You've got your pink tourmaline crystal to protect you, don't you?"

"Ha, ha. No, I left it at home," Pete said. "It kept burning my pocket."

They stepped out of the car into the dark night. Clouds kept covering the moon. Crickets and small night animals loudly reported Pete's and Jupe's every move as they started down the slope into the graveyard. Suddenly Jupe stumbled and went rolling down the hill before Pete could grab him.

"What's the idea of pushing me?" Jupe said when he finally came to a stop.

"I didn't push you," Pete said, hurrying down the slope. "Didn't you trip on something?"

"I don't know," Jupe said, confused.

Somewhere in the distance a dog started barking

and yipping. Then with a single yelp of pain, it stopped. Dead silence.

Pete led the way with his flashlight. "We've got to cross to the other side of the cemetery," he said. "The trucks are probably still parked on the service road there."

They followed their flashlight beams. Jupe aimed his in front, but Pete kept checking behind. He wasn't looking when something came swooping at them. Pete and Jupe felt its breeze and heard its mocking cry.

"What was that?" Pete asked, ducking. "It attacked me."

"An owl," Jupiter answered matter-of-factly. "From its call I'd identify it as a screech owl, indigenous to this area at this time of year."

"Never mind. I wasn't asking for a lecture," Pete said. He pointed with his flashlight in the direction of the service road. "It's over there. You go past an empty grave—that's where they were going to film. The casket should be in the truck marked Special Effects."

"Lead me to it," Jupe said.

"Wait. I thought I heard something."

"Come on," Jupe said, starting ahead.

The grass was smooth and soft under their shoes. The wind brought a thick sweet aroma that seemed to stick to their clothing.

"Wait!" Pete repeated, grabbing Jupe's arm. "I thought I heard something again."

They froze and listened . . . but the cemetery was silent.

"It's your imagination," Jupe said.

"You're not so sure, Jupe. I can hear it in your voice."

"Let's go."

Pete walked on reluctantly, trying to find his way in the dark. Were they in the right row of graves? Yes. They finally came to the freshly dug grave. They stood over it, shining their flashlights into the wet, gaping hole in the ground. But there were no movie trucks. The service road was empty.

"Where are the props and equipment trucks?" Jupe asked.

"They *were* here," Pete said. "Looks like someone moved them."

"Too bad. We came a long way for nothing," said Jupe. He paused. "Did you hear a noise?"

Before Pete could answer, he felt a sharp, stinging blow to the back of his head—and heard Jupe cry out in pain. Pete and Jupe dropped into the open grave like dead men.

9

Cat and Mouse

PETE LANDED WITH A THUD AT THE BOTTOM OF the deep hole. Owww. There was a thumping, thumping in his brain. Where was he? What had happened? Oh, yeah—he had been hit on the back of the head with something heavy. A tree limb, maybe? Was Jupe hurt too?

Pete lifted his head—ow, that felt worse—and saw Jupe lying beside him, not moving. Then he let his head fall back to the soft earth again. A curtain seemed to be closing in front of Pete's eyes, but he fought it, trying to remain conscious. What had happened, again? Wake up, Pete, he told himself. Don't give in. . . .

Then all of a sudden Pete heard a sound and realized something horrible. Whoever had whacked them from behind was still there! He was standing at the edge of the open grave! Pete tried to lift his head, but he couldn't.

Then Pete felt small pieces of something falling on his face.

Oh, no—it's dirt! He's shoveling dirt on us. He's burying us alive!

Someone looked over the edge of the grave. Pete

couldn't see his face, but he saw dull moonlight reflect from the silvery shovel the guy was holding. The figure stepped backward and the dirt began to fall again.

A sound came out of Pete, a screaming, angry sound he couldn't control. *"Noooooo!"*

Pete shook his head hard and rubbed his face with his hand. His hands were muddy from the grave and now his face smelled muddy, too. But the shower of dirt from above stopped.

Pete climbed to his knees and tried to stand up, steadying himself against the narrow walls of the grave. "Jupe! Get up!" Pete called. "Come on, Jupe. We've got to get out of here."

Jupe began to stir, helped by Pete practically lifting him by the shirt front.

"Okay, okay," Jupe said groggily. "Where . . . What . . ." He didn't seem to be able to finish sentences. But he was standing, shaking off the dirt.

Pete let go of Jupe and sprang to his next task. Using his hands and feet to dig and claw in the soft earth, he climbed out of the grave. No one was around. The graveyard was empty except for the crickets and the owls and the dog, who was barking again.

Pete reached down to help Jupe, who came up panting, still too dizzy to do much of the work.

"Come on. Maybe we can catch this guy before he drives off," Pete said.

"No," said Jupe, scraping some of the mud and muck off his shirt. "I think we'll learn more by staying out of sight, so we can follow him."

The headlights of a dark Camaro were just speeding

down the street, heading back toward Los Angeles, as
the two Investigators came up the hill of the cemetery.
Pete climbed behind the wheel of his Vega and took off
a minute later. He wound the little car out as far as he
could in each gear, trying to keep the Camaro in sight.

They followed the Camaro through Huntington
Beach and Long Beach and then on up into L.A.
Then, as they approached a Beverly Hills neighbor-
hood, the area began to look familiar. All too familiar.

"Weren't we just here a few hours ago?" Pete said,
checking out the houses and the street signs they were
passing.

With the help of the streetlights Pete was able to get
a glimpse of the guy driving the Camaro. He looked
young—about nineteen—and he was wearing a white
headband. A moment later the guy made a left turn
into a familiar driveway. It was the driveway of Marble
Ackbourne-Smith.

The front door of Marble's house was still standing
wide open, and the driver of the Camaro went right
in. And so did Pete and Jupe.

In the wee, small hours of the morning, the large
house was dimly lit with candles. Crystals reflected the
candlelight all over. Pete and Jupe walked through
one room after another looking for Marble.

"I feel like a mouse that knows there's a trap," Pete
said.

"Even so, we still want the cheese," added Jupe.

Suddenly a door opened. From a large room lit by
hundreds of flickering candles, Marble emerged with
a man and a woman in their twenties.

"Thank you for seeing us, especially at this late hour," said the man, handing Marble a check. "I see you have more clients."

"Seekers of truth have lost their wrist watch," said Marble, looking quizzically at Jupe and Pete.

"I wish I could write down everything you ever said," said the young woman. "Thank you for contacting my first husband. I had to wish him a happy birthday at midnight. It's a tradition. Thanks again. Good night."

After the two people left, Marble said in a normal voice with a knowing smile, "You didn't find the crystals. I can sense it."

"No, but we have returned from the grave," Jupe said. Pete cracked up.

"We're looking for something else now," Jupe said. "A guy with a white headband."

Marble looked around. "I don't see anyone here like that."

"Try your third eye," Pete said.

"We followed him into your house," Jupe said.

Marble's face changed as though he had just been caught in a lie. "Oh, you must mean Harvey. One of my students. What do you want him for?"

"He tried to bury us alive a little while ago," said Jupe. "He attacked us in Dalton Cemetery when we were looking for Diller Rourke's crystals."

"Harvey?" Marble called softly in the hall. A moment later Harvey, with the white headband, appeared in the doorway.

"That's the guy," Pete said. His hands closed into

fists immediately. "Why were you following us? What did you hit us for?"

"I have been in my room all night," said Harvey.

"That's a lie!" Pete said. "You must have followed us when we left here earlier!"

"I have been in my room all night," Harvey said again. Then he walked backward into his room, never taking his eyes off Marble.

"What's going on around here?" Pete said angrily.

"What goes on in this mellow house is something that will be a mystery to you until you can open your openness," Marble said.

Jupe rolled his eyes. "Oh, please. People always think they can hide things from us," he said. "But my associates and I have always proven them wrong. You're hiding something and I think it has to do with Diller Rourke."

Marble's shoulders shrugged. He didn't say yes. He didn't say no. He changed the subject. "Diller Rourke's disappearance is a heartache to all who know him, including him. He has discovered his openness. He is like that marvelous sculpture called *Finding the Path*. It is a sculpture of four feet, all sharing the same leg and each pointing in a different direction."

Pete suddenly broke in before Jupe could ask his next question. "When was the last time you were at Diller's beach house?"

The question seemed to surprise Marble. "Diller's beach house? I've never been there. The student comes to the teacher."

"Then how did you know about that sculpture

thing, the feet? That sculpture is in Diller's beach house. I saw it there. It was one of the few things that wasn't smashed up."

"How *did* you know about the sculpture?" Jupe asked Marble Ackbourne-Smith.

As if in answer, Marble opened his large, broad hand. In it there was a large light purple crystal. Then he closed his hand again—this time in a tight fist. "I must go to purge the hostile vibrations from my crystals."

Marble called it a night, moving his large body in heavy-footed clumps and leaving Jupe and Pete in the large room where the candles were flickering out one by one.

"Excellent work, remembering the sculpture in Diller's house."

"Stick with me, Jupe. I'll teach you all my tricks," Pete said with a grin.

It was almost two A.M. when they left Marble's house. The night's fresh air made them yawn and remember that it was late.

"I need to catch some z's," Pete said after starting his car. "I'll drop you off."

"What are you going to do with Harvey?" asked Jupe, checking the right side-door mirror. "He's waiting in his car to see where we go."

Pete tensed up and checked the rear-view mirror. Harvey's Camaro was parked a few yards down the block in a shadow behind them. The smile left Pete's face. "If that's the way he wants to play, I'll take it slow and easy so he can keep up with us," Pete said. "Then I'll lose him at Carabunga."

"Sounds good to me," said Jupe as he settled back to enjoy the ride.

"Most people have the wrong idea about how to drive when you know you're being followed," Pete explained.

"Mmmm-huh," Jupe said, his eyes glued to the mirror so he could watch Harvey trailing behind them.

"You got to be a supercourteous driver to the bozo who's following you," Pete went on. "For example, you don't want to speed through any yellow lights. What if he doesn't make the light? He's lost you and the fun is over. And you don't want to play leapfrog changing lanes all the time. That makes him blow his cover to keep up with you."

"Three blocks to Carabunga," Jupe said.

"Let's say good night to Harvey," Pete said. He floored the accelerator and sped the wrong way up a one-way street for one crazy block, grateful that there was no oncoming traffic. Then he made a sharp right turn and bounced his car right up onto the curb. Immediately he shut off the engine and turned out the lights. Then he and Jupe ducked down.

Pete had made a perfect three-point landing in the back row of Carabunga Motors' used car division. They peeked out the side window just in time to see Harvey circling the block.

"He can't find us. He's giving up and driving off," Jupe said.

"Okay, Harvey," Pete said with a laugh as he started the motor. "Now it's our turn to follow you. And you'd better take us someplace interesting."

10

The Third Eye

IT WAS THE FOURTH TIME THAT NIGHT THAT PETE and Jupe had switched places with Harvey in the game of cat and mouse. And the game was getting harder to play. At well past two in the morning, there were so few cars on the streets that Pete had to stay several blocks back just to keep out of sight.

"This better be worth it," Pete said, yawning.

"You know what I've been thinking, Pete?" Jupe said. "Harvey may be leading us right to where Diller is being held."

Pete sat up straighter and edged a little closer to the Camaro. "You think Marble and Harvey are in with the kidnappers?" he asked.

Jupe's answer was blunt and cold. "They're lying about something."

They were in Bel Air now, one of Los Angeles's most exclusive neighborhoods. Suddenly Harvey pulled over and stopped in front of a three-story pink stucco house with a Mexican clay tile roof. In the moonlight a weeping willow tree cast a large shadow, shaped like a stalking cat, against the house.

Harvey got out of his car, scanning the sleeping

neighborhood in every direction. Then he put on a dark backpack and moved cautiously toward the darkened house. It was clear from his movements that he was worried about tripping a security system.

"Whoever is in the house isn't expecting him or he'd knock on the front door," Pete said.

Once they were out of their car, Pete and Jupe were doubly cautious. They didn't want to trigger the security system, either. And they didn't want to be caught by Harvey.

Harvey walked the front perimeter of the house, checking every window. Pete and Jupe planted themselves behind a fat old tree.

"What's he doing?" whispered Pete.

"He seems to be looking in all the windows," Jupe said. "But I don't think anyone is home. And he's talking into a small tape recorder."

When Harvey was done talking, he pulled out a camera and took photos through the darkened windows. Then he got into his car and slipped away, going directly to Marble's house.

"Back where we started from," Pete said, leaning sleepily on the steering wheel with both hands. "What do we do now, Jupe?"

Jupe was sound asleep.

The next afternoon, sitting in Headquarters, Jupe and Pete filled Bob in on the events of the previous night. They covered being pushed into the grave at the cemetery, following and being followed by Harvey, and finally watching Harvey photograph a dark house.

"Dynamite story, guys. Can't wait for the movie. But what's this got to do with Diller? I thought we were trying to find him," Bob said.

"Okay, we didn't find Diller last night, as I had hoped. But we know that Marble has a powerful hold on Diller," Jupe said.

"And Marble lied," Pete said. "He claimed he had never been to Diller's house, even though he knew about that statue that's *in* Diller's house."

"Sculpture, not statue," corrected Jupe. "Anyway, you could be right, Bob. We may be pursuing the wrong man. But other than Richard Faber specifically, and all of Hollywood generally, Mr. Ackbourne-Smith is all we've got."

A knock on the trailer door made everyone freeze for a second. Jupe tucked in his T-shirt before answering the door.

"Hi," said a girl. Her long, frizzy blond hair fell wildly over one side of her face, covering one of her green eyes. "Is Bob here?"

"Uh," Jupe said nervously. He actually couldn't remember and had to look behind him. "Come in," he was finally able to say.

"Hey, Morgan," Bob said, giving the girl a friendly smile.

"Am I early? What is this place?"

"Early?" Bob said. "No, I forgot the time. These are my friends, Jupiter Jones—"

"Great name. Really spacey," said Morgan.

"And Pete Crenshaw," said Bob.

"Hi," Pete said. "What high school?"

"Hollywood High," said Morgan with a smile. She bit her lip when she smiled.

"Morgan's the singer with a group called Jammin' Jelly," Bob said. "I got them booked at a party tonight. So we've got to go."

"Well, thanks for stopping by, Bob," Jupe said.

"Yeah, we were forgetting what you looked like," added Pete.

"Guys, what can I say?" said Bob. "A job's a job." He slipped his arm through Morgan's and led her to the door.

When they were gone, Jupe said, "Did you see her?"

"I was using all three eyes," Pete said.

"Bob gets all the beautiful women without even trying," Jupe said with a sigh. "What am I doing wrong?"

"In a word," said Pete, *"everything!"*

Jupe glared at Pete for a moment, then sighed again. "You're probably right."

The next day was Saturday, and Pete met Jupe and Bob at the beach. November wasn't prime swimming time—except for the die-hard surfers who'd hotdog with both legs in a cast if they had to. But it was still great weather for a little touch football and a bonfire cookout.

"I'm going ten yards out on a crossing pattern. You hit me with a bullet when I buttonhook," Pete said, flipping the football to Jupe.

"Why don't I just throw you the ball?" asked Jupe.

"Sure—whatever makes you happy," Pete said, rolling his eyes. He took off down the beach, then turned around for the pass. But the ball went sailing five yards behind him. "That was a guaranteed interception," he told Jupe as he trotted back with the ball.

"You know," Jupe said absently, "if we don't find Diller Rourke, they're going to have to stop production on *The Suffocation II*."

But Pete wasn't listening. Instead, using his hands to shield his eyes from the late-afternoon sun, he looked a long way down the beach. "Hey, Jupe. I'm going down there by the cement steps."

"Are you kidding?" Jupe looked appalled. "I can't throw that far."

Pete laughed. "I know. But I think I see Kelly over there with a girlfriend."

Pete jogged down the beach, slowing when he got to the steps in the side of the dune. Kelly was sitting with one of her cheerleader girlfriends, who stood up and walked away when she saw Pete coming.

At first Kelly looked like she was going to leave too.

"Hi," Pete said, shifting the football from under one arm to the other.

"Hi," Kelly said.

"How's it goin'?"

Kelly nodded without saying anything.

"I've been thinking about you," he said, spinning the football in his hands. "I was going to call you, but the last week has been crazy. We're working on a case. Kidnapping."

Kelly stared at the football. "Have you challenged the kidnappers to a game of football on the beach?"

"Uh, no. Jupe and I came down to the beach— we're waiting for Bob. We're working on this case. I told you."

Kelly stood up. "I'm working on my own case—the case of the missing boyfriend," she said. She turned over a rock with her foot. "Nope. Not there. I give up."

They looked at each other for a moment. Pete knew it was his turn to say something. But it had to be good.

"Hey, look, babe. I'm not missing. But someone else is. Really. It's important."

Kelly shrugged and looked hurt. "I wish I were important," she said, and ran to catch up with her girlfriend.

Pete walked back up the beach . . . alone. He had hoped he'd be walking back with Kelly beside him. But he wasn't. To make matters worse, Bob had arrived and he'd brought Morgan, the fabulous-looking singer. She was dressed for the beach in iridescent pink tights, a long black T-shirt, and high heels.

"First of all, you guys," Bob said, "Morgan was sensational last night. I think we may have made a deal for a record contract."

"There were all kinds of Hollywood types at the party. Real hamburger heads," Morgan said with a giggle.

"Including—are you ready for this?" Bob said. "Marble Ackbourne-Smith!"

"I've read all his books," Morgan said, twisting a curl of her frizzy hair, which didn't need any more twisting. "A metaphysical minicube, but for a man his age, he looks great in a bathing suit."

"Yeah, Marble went swimming at the party," Bob added.

"But he can't swim!" Pete exclaimed.

"He said it's one way to open his openness," Bob said. "Anyway, six people jumped in the pool to save him. He's quite a showman. He was really working on one particular woman, a very wealthy widow." Bob stopped for a minute. "Pretend this is a crystal in my hand," he said, picking up a smooth white pebble from the beach. He touched the pebble to Morgan's forehead and then to his. "Mrs. Wembly, we have never met, but I feel that our auras are in tune," Bob said, imitating Marble's voice.

Morgan changed to a Southern accent. "Why, ah don't know what you mean," she said.

"I see a Chagall painting hanging in your house," Bob went on. "The old wooden frame has a chip in the lower right corner, probably from being dropped at one time."

"That's absolutely true, darlin'! How could you know that?"

Bob touched Morgan's forehead again with the pebble and closed his eyes. "I see a cute little kitten sleeping in an antique ceramic bowl."

"It's uncanny!" Morgan squealed.

"But here's the clincher," Bob said to Jupe. He touched Morgan's forehead again. "And what an unusual willow tree. It seems to cast a shadow like a cat on your house!"

"Willow tree? Cat shadow?" Pete shouted, and stood up. "Harvey!"

"I thought you'd like our little scene," Bob said as he and Morgan took a dramatic bow.

"So that's it," Jupe said. "Harvey was spying on Mrs. Wembley the other night, gathering information for Marble to use at the party."

"And she was falling for it," Bob said. "She was ready to write him a large check on the spot if he would agree to be her adviser."

"It's quite a clever scam," Jupe said.

"That's how Marble could know about Diller's sculpture but never go to Diller's beach house," Pete said. "Harvey probably photographed it."

"Well, anyway, the guy's a total phony," Bob said. "Although I wouldn't say that to his face. He's big enough to pin me to the mat like a squashed mosquito."

"That's it!" Pete shouted, smacking his forehead again and again. "What a jerk! How could I forget?"

"Forget what?"

"That's where I know Marble from. He's Tommy the Two-Ton Titan! Marble Ackbourne-Smith is a wrestler I used to watch on TV when I was a kid! He used to come into the ring carrying these two black metal weights. They each said 'one ton' on them. He bragged about being the world's strongest, meanest wrestler. I *knew* I'd seen him somewhere before."

Jupe and Bob burst out laughing.

"And here's the worst part," Pete went on. "Before he was a wrestler—he was a champion swimmer!"

All three of them howled.

"The man's entire life has been a total fraud," Jupe said. "From phony wrestling to phony New Age predictions seen with his third eye."

"Yeah, and we know who his third eye is," Bob said. "Harvey."

"Right. But I'm afraid this means that Marble Ackbourne-Smith, alias Tommy the Two-Ton Titan, is not our kidnapper," Jupe said glumly. "We've been on the wrong suspect all along."

Bob agreed. "He's just a guy after people's money."

"But he sure didn't want us to find out," Pete said. "That's probably why he had Harvey follow us and push us into that grave!"

"Here's some more bad news," Bob said. "I made some phone calls and found out that Richard Faber was in Hawaii the day Diller disappeared. So I think he's out of the picture as a suspect."

"So where do we go from here?" Pete asked.

Jupe shrugged. "Back to square one."

It was evening when Jupe, Pete, and Bob returned to the Headquarters trailer with a stack of rented Diller Rourke movies. With no other leads to follow up on, they hoped that the films might provide a clue.

As Jupe mixed up a protein milk shake in the old blender he had repaired, Pete hit the messages button on the telephone answering machine.

Beep! "Hey, guys," said Pete's father, "I thought you'd want to hear the latest. Marty Morningbaum just got a second ransom note. The kidnappers want some big bucks by ten o'clock tomorrow night—or they'll kill Diller Rourke!"

11

Ransom in the Can

T HE WORDS ON THE ANSWERING MACHINE FELT LIKE a metal choker collar around Pete's neck. "They want big bucks or they'll kill Diller," his father had said. Pete swallowed hard and looked at Jupe. I shouldn't have tried to solve this myself, he thought. Now maybe we're running out of time.

"Too bad your dad didn't say where the drop is," said Bob.

"Maybe he doesn't know," Pete guessed.

"I agree," Jupe said. "I suspect that only the kidnappers and Morningbaum know exactly where and how much. But we've got to find out."

"How?" Pete asked. "Marty made it clear he doesn't want us working on this case."

"I am fully aware of that," said Jupe, "but he'll feel differently if he drops a lot of money—and doesn't get anything in return."

"You mean if the kidnappers just take the money . . . and kill Diller anyway?" Bob said.

Jupe nodded. "So we're going to have to persuade Marty to cut us in. To do that, we'll have to hit him where he lives—Espeto's Restaurant."

Bob whistled. "Espeto's!" Pete said. "Jupe, put your

gear-shift in serious. That place is wall to wall movie celebs and Hollywood power players."

"That's why I'm sure we'll find Morningbaum there," said Jupe. "Tomorrow. It's *the* place for Sunday brunch."

"Yeah, but we can't afford a glass of water in a place like that—and a protein milk shake is probably a couple hundred bucks," Pete said.

Jupe's smile announced that he had already considered that fact and had thought of a plan. "We won't necessarily be eating."

The next day at two, Pete drove Jupe and Bob to Espeto's. Jupe had checked that Marty had a reservation. The restaurant itself was a small redwood building surrounded by unusual Japanese trees and a rock garden. The only difference between it and any other Italian restaurant in L.A. was that every car in Espeto's parking lot cost almost as much as the national debt.

Once they were inside the restaurant, it took a minute to adjust to the darkness. At first they couldn't see a thing. Italian opera played on the sound system and warm garlic wafted through the air.

Then someone cleared his throat in the dark. Pete jumped. It turned out to be the maître d', a tall, balding man in a perfectly pressed tuxedo. He was looking at the three teenagers as if something disgusting had walked in. "What, may I ask, are you doing here?" he asked in a calm but poisonous voice.

What's his problem? Pete thought—until he noticed how they were dressed. Bob was wearing his uniform these days—chino pants, oxford shirt, no socks, loafers. Jupe had on a T-shirt that said WHEN THE GOING GETS TOUGH, THE TOUGH GO OUT TO LUNCH. And Pete realized he wasn't dressed much better, wearing a T-shirt from the rock group Speed Limit, which he chose because he thought it made him look like Richard Faber.

"We'd like to see Mr. Marty Morningbaum," Jupe said.

"Do you think he'd like to see you?" asked the headwaiter.

"Tell him it's Pete Crenshaw," Pete said.

The maître d' nodded reluctantly and left. A moment later he returned and led them to Marty Morningbaum's private table. It was near a window facing the Japanese garden. So many portable telephones and fax machines sat on it that there was only room for a small plate of fruit salad. Marty watched the Investigators with his head cocked to one side.

"Hello, Mr. Morningbaum," Pete said.

"I don't like it when I see you in threes," Marty said, shaking his head.

"Mr. Morningbaum, we understand that you received a second ransom note," Jupiter said. "Could we see it, please?"

Marty's hand moved involuntarily toward his sport coat in the direction of his inside pocket. But just as quickly he pulled his hand away. "I told Pete from the first, kid. Stay out of it. No way am I going to risk someone getting hurt—you guys or Diller. And that's my last word."

One of the portable phones on the table began

ringing. Marty grabbed it and started talking as if the Three Investigators didn't exist.

The three friends retreated to the door.

"It's obvious that he has the ransom note," Jupe said.

"Yeah, in his jacket pocket," Pete said. "How are we going to see it?"

Bob was smiling—a sure sign that he either had a plan or he saw a fabulous girl. In this case it was both. A minute later, he hijacked a waitress by blocking her way. She was a gorgeous brunette with three earrings in her left ear.

"How's it going?" Bob asked, switching on the famous Bob Andrews charm to maximum warp. "We don't know each other, but something tells me that if I ask you to do a favor for me—no matter how strange—you're the kind of person who will do it."

"What producer do you want to meet?" she asked with a funny smile.

Bob shook his head. "I want you to spill something on Marty Morningbaum. And then bring his jacket to us in the kitchen."

The waitress looked from Bob to Jupe to Pete. "Marty Morningbaum? Why don't I just cut my throat?" she said. "What are you going to do? Lift his wallet? His address book? You're crazy."

"I'm not a thief," Bob said, giving the waitress a sincere gaze. "And this isn't a joke. The truth is, it's a matter of life and death."

The waitress stared into Bob's eyes and he gave her his best "you're a beautiful girl" grin. Finally she smiled back. "Oh, why not? If I get fired—who cares?

I'm sick of this stupid job anyway," she said. Then she walked away.

Bob, Pete, and Jupe then sneaked into a pantry between the dining room and the kitchen to stay out of sight, waiting, wondering if she'd really do it.

Suddenly they heard glass crashing and three voices all talking at once. The waitress was apologetic. The maître d' was furious. Marty was calm and forgiving.

A moment later she brought the jacket with a large dripping water stain into the kitchen. "Give me a clean towel," she called to a friend.

Jupe took the jacket and reached into the inside pocket. "Bingo," he said, pulling out the ransom note. He unfolded it. It said: "Come to the telephone booth at Gary's Gas Station, Van Nuys Ave. Sunday at ten P.M. One million dollars. Come alone or Diller Rourke is a dead man."

Quickly Bob copied down the note as the waitress frantically blotted up the water on Marty Morningbaum's jacket. Then Jupe put the note back in the jacket pocket. After thanking the waitress, they rushed back to Pete's car and Jupe reread the copied note.

"Does anyone know where Gary's Gas Station is?" Jupe asked.

"I know the place," Pete said. "It's big and it's busy. All the attendants wear roller skates. A lot of people come just for the show."

By eight o'clock that night the Three Investigators were in place across from Gary's Gas Station. It was brightly lit with fluorescent and neon tubes, and Beach Boys records were blasting out of the speaker system. Pete parked across the street in a medical office parking lot and hoped that his Vega wouldn't be too obvious when Morningbaum pulled up.

Then the Three Investigators simply waited and watched. From their vantage point they could see the gas pumps, the roller skaters, and two phone booths. One was near the street, the other one closer to the building.

The two hours dragged by, especially since they knew nothing would happen until ten.

"Why did we have to come so early?" Pete asked Jupe.

"Shh. Limo coming," whispered Bob.

It was 9:58 P.M.

They watched a white stretch Mercedes pull slowly into the gas station and stop by an out-of-order air pump. A rear door swung open and Marty Morningbaum stepped out. He was carrying a large, expensive-looking leather suitcase.

A million dollars. It all fit into one suitcase.

"The note said come alone. I wonder why Morningbaum brought his chauffeur?" Jupe said.

"That *is* alone, in Hollywood!" Bob said.

Marty wrapped his arms around the suitcase and carried it over to the phone booth near the street. It was a tight squeeze inside for him and the suitcase together. The minute he closed the door, at exactly ten P.M., the phone rang.

Morningbaum let the phone ring a couple of times while he swiped at his wet forehead with his palm. He kept looking toward his car.

"What's he waiting for?" Pete asked.

Finally he picked up the phone. The voice on the other end did all of the talking. Marty just kept nodding to everything he was told. Then he hung up.

Pete started the engine of his Vega and slowly rolled out of the parking lot, following Morningbaum's car. It led them to an elementary school in a quiet suburb not far from Bel Air.

"The kidnapper is probably already here," Jupe said softly as they neared the school. "We've got to be quiet."

Pete killed the engine and the lights before his car came to a stop. Then they got out quietly to follow Marty, who was well ahead of them. They stayed in the shadows and watched as Marty dragged the suitcase noisily along the ground on its wheels. He neared the playground equipment.

The night was very cloudy and dark, with only a little moonlight shining. Pete could hardly see. But what he heard was unmistakable.

It was the sound of Marty Morningbaum pulling the lid off a heavy steel trash can in the middle of the playground. Then the suitcase dropped in. With a loud clatter, Marty replaced the lid. That was the drop. A million dollars in a leather suitcase sitting in a trash can.

No one breathed as Marty walked past their hiding place in the bushes. He was close enough that they could smell his after-shave.

"Now we'll see some action," whispered Bob.

"Maybe," Pete said hesitantly.

Waiting was never fun. Especially on a playground. The swings creaked. Was that just the breeze or was something sitting on them? Twigs and branches snapped. Was that the breeze or was someone stepping on them?

Rattle! Crash! A steel garbage can lid. It wasn't the breeze. Someone was picking up the suitcase!

Pete saw a single dim figure a hundred yards away. Moonlight did not reflect off him. He seemed to be wearing black clothes and a black ski mask.

The three teenagers took off running, running as fast as they could. Instantly the dark-clothed figure ran too.

Pete took the lead, stretching out, making every muscle propel him faster and farther. Then, catlike, instant stop! The footsteps in the darkness in front of him had stopped.

"Spread out!" Pete called to Bob and Jupe in a loud voice. Let's make this guy think there are fifteen of us, not three, he thought to himself.

Somewhere to the left, the footsteps started again. Pete took off running, around the swings, past the seesaws. Running and listening. Then he stopped to listen harder. Silence. Where were Jupe and Bob?

The suitcase must be slowing him down. Or he's getting tired, Pete thought. Or he's gone.

Smack! A dizzying pain caught Pete right in the stomach. Suddenly there was no air. His lungs gasped, his gut ached. Then Pete fell straight over on his stomach and lay there in a heap—totally unable to breathe.

12

Inside Job

THE NEXT THING PETE KNEW THERE WERE FOOT-steps coming toward him in the dirt. He tried to stand up, but someone large was standing over him. It was too dark to see faces—or was he blacking out? A pair of hands yanked him to a sitting position and shook him a little.

"Pete, are you okay?"

It was Jupe. He sounded worried.

"What happened?" Bob asked.

Pete shook his head hard.

"I got hit in the stomach," Pete said. "I never even got a chance to karate-chop him! I think I got hit with a million dollars in a suitcase. Whatever it was, it creamed the wind out of me. I couldn't breathe."

"The kidnapper got away. You were running around like a madman and by the time Bob and I caught up with you, he was gone," Jupe said.

"How do you feel?" asked Bob."

"I feel . . . hungry," Pete said.

"He's back to normal," Bob said to Jupe.

In a little while Pete, Jupe, and Bob were standing in line at the nearest Smarty's Food Restaurant. Pete ordered a double beef 'n' cheese IQ Burger. Bob ordered an apple fritter. And Jupe criticized the name of the restaurant.

"Do you realize it's ridiculous calling this place Smarty's?" he asked the girl who was trying to take his order. "*Food* Restaurant? What other kind of restaurant is there? That's not smart—that's redundant."

"Where'd you escape from, Chuck?" the girl asked.

"Jupiter," said Jupe, sharply correcting her.

"That's what I thought," she said. "You want something to eat, Chuck?"

When Jupe finally joined Bob and Pete at a table, he was sipping something in a tall plastic cup.

"That looks suspiciously like a strawberry milk shake," Bob said as Jupe sat down.

"She told me it's their protein milk shake," Jupe said. "They do them differently here."

"I guess putting in a floater of ice cream qualifies as doing them differently." Bob laughed.

Jupe cleared his throat. "Let's talk about something more important," he said. "The kidnapper. The pickup guy. There was something familiar about him."

"I know this: He swings a mean suitcase," Pete said. "I'm lucky he didn't bust a few ribs."

"Did it feel like the suitcase was swung in a downward or an upward arc?" Jupe asked.

"Who cares? It hurt!" Pete complained.

"All I meant was, is he tall or short?"

Pete took a big bite of his burger. The ketchup oozed out, reminding him of blood. "He didn't seem short when we were chasing him."

"I agree," Jupe said.

"That makes three of us," Bob said.

"So now we know that there is something familiar about him and that he's tall," Jupe said.

"Well, that eliminates Richard Faber once and for all," Pete said. "He looks tall in the movies, but I met him and he's puny. Strong, but puny."

"Well, then who?" asked Bob.

Pete shrugged. Jupe pulled out the copy of the second ransom note again, looking for a clue he might have missed. Suddenly he stopped drinking his strawberry shake and closed his eyes.

"Wait a minute," Jupe said, his eyes popping open. He suddenly grabbed Pete's half-eaten burger on its small plastic tray and put it in the middle of the table. Next he put the salt shaker near the burger. He set the pepper farther away, close to the edge of the table.

"Look at the ransom note," Jupe said excitedly, although he didn't wait long enough for Pete or Bob to read it. "It says to come to the telephone booth at Gary's Gas Station. Okay, this is Gary's Gas Station." He pointed to the burger on the table. "These are the two phone booths," he said, pointing to the salt and pepper shakers. "One was near the building and one was near the street. Follow me?"

"Yeah, but I don't know where you're going," said Pete.

"You will. One more minute," Jupe said. "Now, what happened when Morningbaum arrived?"

"He got out of his car and went into a phone booth," Pete said, pointing to the pepper shaker.

"And the phone rang," added Bob.

"Exactly!" said Jupe, picking up the pepper shaker. "We didn't see him think or choose or flip a coin. And the note didn't tell him *which phone booth to go into!* But he went straight into that particular phone booth—and it rang! How did he know which one the kidnappers would call?"

No one said anything for a minute. Pete was amazed, as usual, by his friend's brilliant brain.

"Maybe it was a lucky guess," suggested Bob.

"A possibility, of course," Jupe agreed. "But the other possibility is that Marty Morningbaum knew to go into that phone booth—because he's somehow involved with the kidnapping!"

Bob stood up.

"Where are you going?" Pete asked.

"To make a phone call," Bob said.

His two friends looked at him.

"I'm supposed to meet Morgan in half an hour at an all-night recording studio," Bob explained. "But Jupe has that 'let's go search someone's private office' look on his face. So I figure I'd better reschedule the session."

At one in the morning the Three Investigators drove up to the movie studio in a truck that belonged to Jupe's uncle's junkyard. They stopped a block away from the tall, arched iron studio gates to get organized and get their story straight.

"Cool place. Needs flags," said Morgan, who was sitting next to Bob in the back of the truck. The belt on her black leather pants glowed in the dark.

"Most girls take a guy's word for it when he says he has to break a date," Jupe grumbled.

"I don't settle out of court for anything," Morgan said. "Besides—I knew Bob wouldn't cancel unless he had something cool to do. So I said to myself, why should I miss out?"

"Okay, I'm going to the gate," Pete said. "Everyone get down under the covers."

As soon as Bob, Jupe, and Morgan were hidden under a tarp, Pete drove to the gate and stopped by the guardhouse.

"Pete Crenshaw?" said the surprised guard. "What are you doing here? It's one A.M."

"My dad got one of Marty Morningbaum's famous midnight calls ordering him to get in here and haul his stuff off the Suffocation set," Pete said. "But he was too beat, so I'm helping him out."

"Yeah, I hear they're closing up shop. But nobody called me about you," said the guard, staring at Pete.

Play it cool, Pete told himself as he held his breath. He didn't say anything. Just waited for the guard to decide.

"Well, since it's you, okay, go on and get your stuff. Maybe you'll get some sleep tonight."

"Thanks," Pete said, putting the truck in gear. Once he was past the guardhouse, he let out a long breath and wound his way through the studio lot to the small building where Marty Morningbaum had his office.

"Morgan, we need you to stand guard for us from the truck," Bob said, hopping out. "If you hear the security cops coming, lay on the horn."

"Stay here?" Morgan said. She giggled and shook her head. "No way. I didn't bring enough gum."

Jupe glared at Bob again and Morgan saw him.

"Oh, lighten up, fudgeface," she said, pinching Jupe on the cheek.

Jupe almost growled.

Meanwhile Pete had found an unlocked window. Five minutes later he was inside, opening the front door for his friends.

"Hurry up," he whispered. "The security guard is on his way through."

Once they were inside Marty Morningbaum's office, Jupe took over. "Okay. We're looking for something to connect Marty to that phone booth or to the kidnappers. It could be written on a scrap of paper or even something that looks like code. Let's get to work."

The three mini-flashlight beams spread out in three different directions. Jupe checked the file cabinets. Bob checked the trash cans. Pete looked through Marty's desk.

And Morgan sang as she walked around opening closets. Suddenly she stopped. "Anyone here have a camera?" she asked. Bob rushed over to her.

"Why? Did you find something?" he said.

"No, I just felt like having my picture taken," she said.

"Sorry, guys," Bob said in a low voice.

"Scripts, contracts, budgets," Jupe said, naming the contents of the file cabinets. "Zip."

"All I'm finding in the trash are phone messages that say 'Let's do lunch,' " Bob said.

Pete looked down at Marty's desk. There was something here to find—Pete had that feeling.

He opened the first drawer of Marty's desk. In the beam of his flashlight he saw a dozen different watches, plus pills, a comb, a toothbrush, gold-plated golf tees, and a photo of Marty, Diller, and Marble Ackbourne-Smith. There was a bull's-eye drawn around Marble.

Pete closed the desk drawer and opened another. It was empty. That was strange. Then he looked at the telephone. It had four phone lines and a row of buttons for special features. Bingo! That was it!

"Hey, Jupe. There's a redial button."

Jupe stopped what he was doing and came over. "I wonder who he called last?" Jupe said.

"Do it," Bob said to Pete. "Push the button."

Pete picked up the receiver. A light lit. He pushed the redial button.

Boop-boop-beep-boop-beep-boop-beep! The phone dialed the last number that had been called from that phone. It began to ring.

"Yeah," said a voice at the other end. "Marty? Is that you?"

Pete's tongue froze. His whole body went numb. He recognized the voice!

"Hello? Who is it?" the voice on the other end said. But Pete couldn't answer. His mind was swirling. He slammed the phone down on the cradle.

"What's wrong with you!" said Jupe. "Who was it? Who answered the phone?"

"You aren't going to believe this," Pete said, shaking. "I know that voice. It was Diller Rourke!"

13

Jupe Cuts Up

OF COURSE IT WAS DILLER ROURKE—IT HAD TO BE. Pete had seen enough of Diller's movies to recognize that throaty, tough-guy tone of voice anywhere.

"Tell me again," Jupe said. "You hit the redial button, the phone rang, and Diller Rourke answered the phone?"

"Right."

Pete, Jupe, and Bob locked eyes. They were all coming to the same conclusion.

"So the last person Marty Morningbaum called from this phone was Diller," Bob said. He thought for a minute, then grabbed the phone and hit the redial button again. He waited. His lips moved as he counted the number of rings to himself. "No answer," he announced finally.

"All right," Jupe said. "Fact number one—Diller Rourke has not been kidnapped at all."

"Or if he has," said Bob, "he's the first kidnap victim to be given phone privileges."

Morgan giggled and then looked apologetically at Jupe. "I think he's funny. So sue me. My stepfather's a lawyer." She sat down on Marty's desk and swung her legs.

"Fact number two," said Pete, sitting down in Marty's executive chair. "Marty knows where Diller is."

"Unless someone *else* used this phone to call that number where Diller answered."

It was Morgan, popping her gum and offering her own analysis.

"Possible," Jupe said grudgingly.

"But not too likely," Pete chimed in. "Diller just now called me Marty on the phone."

"Right," Jupe said to Pete. "I think we can assume Marty has known where Diller is all along."

"So what we're saying is that Marty and Diller probably planned this kidnapping together—everything: the disappearance, messing up his house, the ransom notes," said Bob. "But why?"

That big question mark stopped them cold.

"Yeah," said Morgan. "I mean, really, why would Hollywood's hottest hunk and Marty Morningbaum torpedo a movie like *The Suffocation II*? It's going to sell a lot of popcorn."

"Let's keep looking," Jupe said, rifling the desk papers again. "Maybe the answer is here."

All of a sudden the lights snapped on. Everyone froze and turned toward the door. Standing there with one hand on the light switch and one hand on his billy club was a security guard. "Hey! What are y'all doin' in here?" he drawled. He was a young Southerner, tall and scarecrow thin. His security guard hat was pushed back on his pale forehead and a straw-colored shock of yellow hair poked forward.

Pete looked at Jupe, who looked at Bob, who looked at Pete.

"I said what's going on in here?"

"Pete," said Bob, "it's your turn to explain."

"Huh-uh," Pete said. "I explained the last time. It's Jupe's turn." Pete pointed at Jupe.

The guard had started off nervous but now confusion was setting in. "Now, y'all aren't supposed to be in here, I know that. And I think I'm supposed to call for backup. Or am I supposed to subdue you first?"

Something in the guard's hesitant manner seemed to give Jupe a clue. He quickly assumed his most adult and authoritative voice. "Officer, I'm going to need your name and badge number. The fact is, this has been a test," Jupe said.

"It has?" the young guard said nervously.

"Yes. As you must know, at this security company we periodically test our agents in real situations. We have been waiting in this office for an hour," Jupe lied. As he spoke he was still fingering through the things in Marty Morningbaum's desk drawers.

"An hour and seven minutes," Bob chimed in, trying to look official as he checked his watch. "I know how you are about accuracy, J.J."

"That is a long time to go undiscovered," Jupe said.

"Are you sure it's been that long?" asked the guard, pulling nervously at his chin.

"You are going to have a lot of explaining to do at the main office." Jupe took a sheet of paper out of Marty's desk. He waved it at the guard. "This is our report and it's not very favorable to you."

"Wait a minute." The guard's face changed. "Look, you guys, I need this job. I didn't know they were running a drill tonight."

"You're not supposed to know," Jupe said. "You're only supposed to do your job."

"How about another chance?" the guard asked, looking at Morgan. "I just started this job."

"What do you say, guys? Let's give him a break," Morgan said.

With a small nod of his head, Jupe tore up the paper. "We expect better performance from you next time," he said as he led the way out of Marty's office.

"Sure thing," the young man said, calling to them. "From now on, I'm on the case. No one gets in or out of here, believe you me."

Outside, as the four teenagers walked back to the truck, Morgan slipped her arm through Jupe's. "Pretty swift dancing in there," she told him.

It was too dark for her to see him blush.

"As a matter of fact," Jupe stammered, "and I hate to admit this—"

"You hate to admit anything," Bob teased.

"But I'm afraid I got carried away and tore up this letter," Jupe said, showing them the paper he had torn. "After that, I couldn't just leave it in Marty's desk."

"Is it an important letter?" Pete asked.

"I think so, but I'm not sure why," Jupe said. "It's a letter from an insurance company and it's about the insurance policy on the filming of *The Suffocation II*. It says here that the company agrees to pay twenty million dollars to Marty Morningbaum, the sum he has spent so far on the movie. Producers regularly take out insurance policies such as this to protect their investment in case the star dies or becomes unable to continue the film. Since Diller has not been available to complete the picture, the insurance company will have to make good on its policy."

"So that's it," Pete said, although he wasn't sure he understood. "Morningbaum set up this fake kidnapping so he could collect on the insurance?"

Jupe shook his head and bit his lower lip. "It doesn't quite compute," Jupe said. "This way, they only make back their twenty million dollars, and no movie comes out. But the first Suffocation picture grossed over two hundred million. The insurance money is small potatoes compared to the potential profits if they finish *The Suffocation II*."

"Hey—where *is* Diller?" asked Morgan.

The Three Investigators looked at each other questioningly. "Let's ask Marty Morningbaum," Jupe suggested.

Bob shook his head. "He won't tell us."

"*We* won't ask him," Jupe said. "Diller will." Jupe was good at doing voices and impersonations. He changed his voice to sound like Diller Rourke. "Marty, this is Diller. Come quick. I'm in trouble," Jupe said.

"Close, but no cigar," Pete said. "You could fool a lot of people, but not Marty, I don't think. The only thing that will get him to come is Diller's own voice."

"Diller's own voice," Jupe said slowly, and clicked

his tongue several times. "I'll bet that can be arranged."

Jupe's idea was a brilliant one, which he pointed out as he explained it to his friends. He reminded Pete and Bob that they had encountered some spliced audio tape on a case in Mexico recently.

"Now we can put that little trick to work ourselves," said Jupe. He went on to explain that when movies are made, the picture is recorded on film, but the sound is recorded separately on quarter-inch audio tape. Later it is converted to a 35mm reel of audio tape and then synchronized with the film in the editing process.

"So all we have to do is get the sound reels from the dailies and we can edit Diller's voice to say anything we want. Then we'll leave Diller's message on Marty's answering machine."

Pete agreed—it was a brilliant idea. Bob was excited and Jupe was practically floating. So it was too bad that Pete had to burst Jupe's balloon.

"There's only one problem, Jupe. The sound reels are *locked* in a vault. We're talking major breaking and entering. Safecracking, even. Forget it."

Jupe's face fell.

"But don't worry. We don't need the dailies," Pete went on. "Why don't we use the stack of Diller Rourke videotapes we rented? They're back at Headquarters, remember? We can dub the sound tracks onto audio tape and edit them that way."

Jupe gave Pete one of his rare admiring smiles as the four of them got inside the truck.

The lights at the Three Investigators' headquarters burned all night. Jupe and Pete watched Diller Rourke movies while Bob took Morgan home. By the time Bob returned, Jupe had recorded several lines of Diller's movie dialogue onto a separate open-reel tape.

"Diller's best movies are adventure films, but they aren't the best for our purposes," Jupe informed Bob. "We got most of these lines from the one comedy Diller made. It's called *Gorilla Teacher*."

"Yeah," Pete chimed in. "Diller works in this science lab with gorillas and as an experiment he substitutes one for a high school dean and no one realizes they made a switch."

Then Jupe started editing the dialogue. Diller telling the gorilla "You're a real smarty" soon became just the word "Smarty." Then, with a grease pencil, Jupe marked where the sound of the *s* began and ended on the tape. He cut it away with a razor blade. When the tape was spliced back together, they had Diller saying "Marty."

Soon the sentences "I need to think about this" and "Thanks for your help" became Diller saying "I need your help."

It was seven in the morning on Monday when their tape was finally done. They called the answering machine in Marty Morningbaum's office.

"This is Marty," said the machine. "I'm in a hurry, so leave a quick message and I'll talk to you ASAP. *Beep!*"

Jupe turned on his tape player and held the phone

up to a speaker. Diller's voice came through loud and clear.

"Marty, I need your help. Come as fast as you can!" Diller's voice said.

Jupe hung up the phone quickly.

"Let's get over to the studio fast—and *hope* that Morningbaum doesn't call his machine from somewhere else," Jupe said. "He should be into work soon, but he won't stick around for long, not after he hears that message. He'll probably call Diller, but I'm betting that Diller won't answer the phone anymore. He can't risk it—not after Pete's call to him last night. So if my plan works, Marty will have to go straight to Diller's hideout—and *we'll* go along for the ride!"

14

No Loss!

M ARTY MORNINGBAUM'S CAR, A GLEAMING, WAXED black Porsche Cabriolet, pulled out of the movie studio lot about noon. He was traveling. He didn't slow down to wave at the guard. He didn't check the traffic before he pulled out. His screeching tires as he stomped on the gas were his only warning to oncoming cars that he was making a left turn, whether anyone liked it or not.

Pete's hands flexed in readiness on the hard plastic of his small Vega's steering wheel. He was parked across the street, watching Morningbaum speed off. "I think he got our message," Pete said.

"More importantly," Jupe said with a smile, "he fell for it."

Pete pulled away from the curb, keeping his car at a safe distance from the Porsche, blending in with the other traffic. They followed Marty north until L.A. and the heavy traffic were far behind them. The landscape became flat farmlands. After a while, Morningbaum turned off the main road, taking narrower and rougher roads that led up into the coastal mountains. Pine trees and redwoods were everywhere. When Morningbaum turned onto a private dirt road, a dead end, Pete stopped the car and killed the engine. They were three hours from L.A.—and the chase was over.

The Three Investigators waited in their car for five minutes to be sure they could walk up the road unseen. Then they made the hike. There was a log cabin around the bend. A trail of black smoke puffed from the chimney. What were Diller and Marty doing in there? Pete wondered. Had Diller already told Marty that he didn't make that phone call?

"That fire looks good," Pete said, rubbing his hands together. It was cold in the mountains and the Three Investigators were just wearing T-shirts.

"Back door?" Bob asked.

"Let's surprise them at the front," said Jupe.

When they got to the front door, Pete counted off quietly. Then all at once, with a shout, the three teenagers kicked the door open. They leaped into the log cabin, expecting to finally see Diller.

But Diller wasn't there.

Instead they found a large, sparsely furnished room. What furniture there was—a dining table, chairs, a couch, a small bookcase—had been cut out of the same logs as the cabin.

In the middle of the cabin's vast living room Marty Morningbaum was jogging on an exercise treadmill. He looked different now, however. The worried look, the tired, defeated eyes, the gray sickly skin, were all gone. He looked pleased to see the Three Investigators come crashing through his door.

"Boys, boys, boys, what's going on, boys?" Marty

said paternally. He pushed a button on his watch and stopped jogging long enough to wipe his face with the towel around his neck.

The Three Investigators ignored the question and spread out, searching the cabin for Diller. But it didn't take long to see that Diller simply wasn't there.

"What are you boys doing here?" asked Marty. He didn't sound at all surprised to see them. "Why, I'd almost think you followed me."

"We've been hiking in the woods," Pete said.

"Looking for snakes," Bob added, staring coldly at Morningbaum.

"How about some doughnuts?" Marty asked cheerfully.

"Doughnuts?" Pete looked at Jupe. "What's going on?"

Jupe shrugged, and Marty beamed. He was being friendlier than ever. "Of course, I never touch them myself, all that fat," Marty said. "But something told me that I was going to have guests today. So I brought some from the commissary. And here you are. What a coincidence."

"Whose cabin is this?" asked Jupe.

Marty's watch beeped and he started jogging on the treadmill again. "It's mine," he said, puffing a little. "It's where I come to recharge."

"Are you alone?" Jupe asked.

"Certainly not," Marty said.

Pete held his breath and glanced around.

"No, you're never alone with nature," Marty said. "Fresh air. Trees. Wild animals. They're all around.

I can stand them for about thirty-six hours. Then I run back to the city."

He stopped jogging again and stepped off the treadmill. He wiped his face and it was almost as if he had smeared on a large grin with the towel. "Boys, you don't look happy. What's wrong?"

"We know you got a message on your answering machine today," Jupe said. "You thought it was from Diller Rourke asking you for help. That's why you came up here. You knew Diller was here."

"Diller staying here?" Marty laughed triumphantly. "It's a great story, boys, but take a look around. Does it look like anyone's been here in months? Go ahead, look."

He was making it a challenge. But he was right. The floor and all the furniture were dusty. Jupe scratched his head.

"My dad has a dozen spray cans of this stuff in our basement," Pete said angrily. "You can't fool me with special effects."

"You boys have great imaginations," Marty said, shaking his head. "But you're wrong. I didn't get any messages today. You can listen to my answering machine if you want. No messages. I came up here to celebrate."

"Celebrate what?" Pete asked.

"Celebrate Diller's release, of course. Don't look so surprised, boys. Haven't you heard the good news? The ransom was paid and the kidnappers let Diller go—just as I knew they would."

Surprised was putting it mildly.

"When did this happen?" Jupe said.

"A few hours ago. Just before I left L.A.," Marty said. He walked to the pantry area and opened up a box of doughnuts. Then he started taking out glasses. "Have some milk. You've still got a lot of growing to do—growing and learning." He was having a great time.

"Does this mean that now you'll be able to finish *The Suffocation II*?" Jupe asked.

Marty laughed quietly. It was the first flicker of surprise he had shown. "You know, unfortunately, because so much time has gone by, I'm going to have to close down *The Suffocation II*. But what can I do? Diller's very shaken up, as you can imagine, and now it's too late. The other actors are committed to other movies. Besides, the movie stank. Jon Travis couldn't direct his way out of a paper bag."

"I see," Jupe said slowly. It was light bulb time for Jupe and it showed. "You *don't want* to finish the film! You realized it was going to be a bomb, so you decided to collect the twenty million dollars instead."

"Collect twenty milllion bucks?" asked Marty, pouring glasses of milk. "Boys, *The Suffocation II* cost me a bundle."

"But you're going to get it back. The insurance company will have to pay you twenty million for not finishing the movie," Jupe said.

One of the glasses dropped from Marty's hand and shattered on the floor. Broken glass. *Crunch, crunch*. "You guys know more about the movie business than I thought," he said. "But no use crying over spilled

milk. You're right. The insurance is covering my
losses on the film. That's what insurance is for. Boys,
there's nothing wrong with that."

"There's something wrong with faking a kidnapping
long enough to collect the insurance money," Jupe
said harshly. "It's called fraud."

Marty stared at them coldly. "Saying it is one thing.
Proving it's another. I think you'd better leave now.
This conversation is over."

As they drove back to the city Pete turned on the
heater, but he still felt cold. Jupe kept checking his
watch, saying he wanted to see the five o'clock news. At
about ten minutes till five, when they were still a long
way from Rocky Beach, Jupe spotted a dilapidated old
diner at the side of the road. It was a sorry sight except
for one thing: It had a large satellite dish in back.

"Pull in here," Jupe insisted, jumping out of the car
before it stopped.

There were no customers in the diner—just a cook
standing with a plate of scrambled eggs in one hand
and a fork in the other.

"How about watching the news?" Jupe asked.

The man kept scooping eggs into his mouth as he
nodded toward the TV. So Jupe quickly flipped it on
and found the *Five-Alarm News*.

"Some actors portray heroes, but today one actor
proved that he *was* a hero," the TV anchorperson said
into the camera. "This morning police found young
and popular movie actor Diller Rourke wandering the
streets in a dazed condition. He told police that he had
just been released after eleven days of being held

captive. And a little while ago he repeated the story of his ordeal in a press conference. A *Five-Alarm News* reporter was there. . . ."

Then the videotape rolled, showing Diller, looking tense, sitting behind microphones at a table in police headquarters. His famous blue eyes were hidden behind sunglasses. Never known for being polite or patient with reporters, Diller was clearly under a lot of strain.

"Did you give a complete description of the kidnappers to the police?" one reporter asked.

"Uh, sure. I said he looked just like you," Diller replied with hostility. "No, Mack. I didn't describe them. I don't know what those jerks looked like. They kept me blindfolded all day, and the room was totally black all night. I never saw anyone."

"Diller, will you and Victoria Jansen get back together now?"

"Will someone throw that jerk out of here?" Diller said. "You know, man, when you're tied up for eleven days, who's dating who just doesn't ring your chimes anymore."

"How many kidnappers were there?"

"I told you. I never saw them."

"Anyone can count the number of voices," Jupiter said, shaking his head. "He's using his acting ability to keep people off-guard."

"Guess what?" Bob said. "It's working."

"Did they hurt you?" a reporter asked.

"No, we all had a picnic." Diller sort of laughed. "You guys are amazing. You want all the gory details, don't you, you vultures? Fine. They tied me up, they beat me, and I screamed my jerkin' head off. I hope they choke on their ransom money just like I hope you choke on your questions."

Diller answered a few more questions and then walked away from the microphones. The police believed him and the reporters believed him. In fact, everyone watching the news that evening believed him—except the three young detectives sitting in the empty diner. But they couldn't think of a way to prove that Diller and Marty Morningbaum were lying.

After the news, Pete drove his friends home, not saying anything for a long time. Finally he exploded.

"We blew it!" Pete yelled. He slapped the steering wheel, accidentally blowing the horn. "They're going to get away with it. How could I play it so wrong?"

It took Jupe a long time to answer. "I'm not sure we were wrong," Jupe said. "Perhaps just outsmarted. Marty and Diller must have had a telephone signal worked out. In any case, they sure didn't fall for our answering-machine trap, did they? No, we were outsmarted—it's as simple as that."

"You can call it whatever you want," Bob said. "It still doesn't feel good."

When they hit Rocky Beach, Pete dropped off Bob and Jupe and then drove around for a while, circling Kelly's neighborhood. He couldn't stop thinking about the case. Would it have been different if he had called Jupe in earlier? There was no way to know.

Finally he jumped out of his car, leaving the headlights on. He ran up and knocked on Kelly's door.

Soon the porch light came on and the door opened. Kelly stood there, looking at him through the screen door.

"Hi," he said.

"Hello, stranger. Don't I know you? Are you lost or something?" Kelly said. "This is my house—where *I* live. Not detective headquarters or the car shop—where *you* live."

Pete opened the screen door. "Come on out. Let's talk."

"You talk. I'm listening," Kelly said, pouting. But she stepped outside onto the porch and stood close to Pete.

"Hey, I don't want to fight. I'm sorry about what happened, okay?" Pete's hands suddenly felt like they weighed a ton. "Sometimes no matter what I do, it doesn't come out right, but that doesn't mean I don't try."

Kelly looked at him strangely. "What's wrong, Pete? I mean, I've never heard you sound so pushed out of shape."

Pete dug into his jeans pocket and pulled out the crystal that Marble Ackbourne-Smith had given him. He put it in Kelly's hand.

"What's this?" she asked.

"Something I don't want anymore," Pete said.

"Why not?"

"Because it reminds me of the one case I tried to handle by myself—and I really blew it."

15

The Vampire Returns

TWENTY-FOUR HOURS LATER, PETE WAS STILL FEEL-ing lousy about the Diller Rourke case. And Jupe wasn't much better. He was trying to drown his sorrows—in hot fudge.

Pete watched the spoon travel up and down, back and forth, from the hot fudge sundae to Jupiter Jones's mouth. In the background the jukebox was shaking the walls of the Ice Creamery with fifties rock.

"Jupe, that's your second sundae," said Pete.

Jupe's eyes looked up from the tall glass sundae dish, but the spoon didn't stop and his head didn't move.

Suddenly the bells on the front door jingled and Bob came into the Ice Creamery. He quickly pulled up a chair. "Hey, guys," he said. "I've got big news. Sax Sendler got an early-morning call—guess who from?"

Jupe shrugged. "I'm not very good at solving mysteries these days," he said.

"Are you ready for this?" Bob said. "Jon Travis called bright and early. He's giving a welcome-back party for Diller Rourke tomorrow night at his house. He wants Morgan's band,"

"That's great for Morgan," Pete said.

"Boys, boys, boys," Bob said, imitating Marty Morningbaum's voice in his cabin the day before. "What I'm trying to say is that this might be our chance to get the truth out of Diller."

"Have we been invited to this party?" Jupe asked.

"Do you think we should let a minor detail like that stop us?" Bob asked with a smile. "Here's my plan. We wear white shirts, black pants, and black bow ties, and sunglasses—and hope that the catering service Travis hired will bring waiters who are dressed like us. Then we blend into the scenery—and mingle, boys, mingle!"

Pete laughed and Jupe actually stopped eating long enough to smile.

The party was in full swing by nine P.M. the next night when Jupe, Bob, and Pete arrived at Travis's Bel Air house. They found the back door and went in through the kitchen to grab some trays of food. No one really noticed them among the other temporary waiters who were rushing in and out carrying trays of hot hors d'oeuvres.

"Okay. Let's circulate through the crowd until we find Diller," Pete said.

Jon Travis's house was a monument to an obsession with gothic horror. The furnishings were heavily carved antiques, upholstered in dark red velvet. The rooms were lit by tall candelabra and wrought-iron sconces holding tapered candles. A large banner that said WELCOME BACK, DILLER! in drippy red paint hung over a casket draped in red roses in the middle of the living room.

Morgan's band was playing outside on the terrace overlooking the pool. The house was filled with Hollywood celebs and movie people eating and dancing in every room.

"There's Morningbaum," Bob said loudly to be heard over the music. "If he spots us, just walk the other way."

"I don't see Diller yet," said Jupe, dodging to avoid another waiter.

Someone suddenly reached over and grabbed some food off Pete's tray. Then he grabbed Pete's sunglasses off his face.

"What's the joke?" Jon Travis asked.

"Uh, hi, Mr. Travis," said Pete. After that, Pete was stuck. He didn't know what to say.

"The detective business wasn't working out so we thought we'd try catering," Bob said, coming to the rescue.

"Well, stay out of the movie business unless you want your heart sliced into little pieces with a scalpel," Travis said.

"What do you mean, Mr. Travis?" asked Jupe.

"I mean, I threw this whole party for Diller, hoping he'd come back and finish *The Suffocation II*. But you know what he said? *Ciao. Au revoir. Hasta luego. Shalom*. And that's 'kiss off' in any language. The little jerk."

"Do you know where Diller is?" Jupe asked.

"At the bottom of my pool if I get my way," Travis said. "But try my torture chamber. I saw him going in there with Victoria Jansen."

Jon Travis pointed the way down a circular stairway to a dark room where he kept his collection of antique torture devices.

Everything in the room seemed to have chains for stretching, spikes for jabbing, or weights for squashing. There the Investigators found Diller and Victoria sitting side by side on the stretching rack, talking to each other.

"Oh, Dill, here are the three detectives who were looking for you," Victoria said, giving the Investigators a friendly smile.

Diller's expression wasn't so friendly as he looked the trio over. "Hi," he mumbled.

"That kidnapping must have been rough," Bob said.

"Yeah," Diller said calmly. "You've really got to be into your openness to cope. You're the guys who've been harassing Marble, huh?"

"Harassing?" Pete said. "Hey, I used to be a big fan of his Saturday afternoon wrestling show."

"We'd like to ask you a couple of questions, since the kidnappers are still at large," Jupe said. "At the press conference you said you couldn't tell how many kidnappers there were. Did you ever count the voices you heard?"

Diller shook his head. "They kept changing their voices," he said. "Just to play with my head, you know." His eyes didn't blink. He was totally cool.

"Would you imitate one of their voices?" Jupe asked.

"Hey, look, chubby . . ." Diller - said, hopping down from the medieval torture device.

But Victoria put her hand on his shoulder. "They're trying to help, Dill," she said.

"It should be easy for you, since you're an *actor*," Jupe said, emphasizing the last word. "Could you say, 'Hello, Marty? Is that you, Marty?' as one of the kidnappers. And then say it again as yourself. I believe it would be very useful."

"Go ahead, Dill. Help them," Victoria said.

Diller said the words. He said them twice, once in a strange voice and once in his own. Pete shivered. Diller's voice was exactly the same as the one he'd heard when he hit the redial button in Morning-baum's office. Pete nodded at Jupe, who nodded back.

"We saw the photo of you tied up," Jupiter said. "Did they keep you tied most of the time?"

Diller was wearing a loose-fitting short-sleeved turquoise shirt. He looked down at his wrists, which were not bruised, and then looked carefully at Jupe. "No, not tied up. Just locked up."

He dodged that one. He's good, Pete thought.

"What was all the glass?" Pete asked.

"What glass?" Diller asked.

"All the glass in your beach house," Pete said. "It was everywhere I looked."

Suddenly all the lights in the house flashed off and on, off and on.

"Hey, everyone into the screening room," Jon Travis announced over a P.A. system. "I've got a surprise."

"Let's go," Diller said to Victoria. "These guys are giving me bad vibes."

"But what about the glass?" Pete asked.

"Hey, man, they grabbed me and threw some kind of bag over my head," Diller said, pushing past the three teenagers. "For all I know, they painted the place red. I haven't been back. You guys better learn to relax." He led Victoria up the circular staircase out of the torture chamber.

"I believe we succeeded in making him nervous," Jupe said when they had gone.

Pete looked around at all the torture devices. "Who wouldn't be nervous down here?"

"We don't need him to be nervous," Bob said. "We need him to make a mistake. But he's too cool. He's going to get away with it."

By the time they got upstairs Jon Travis was standing in front of a large movie screen in his screening room.

"Well, we're all here for the same reason: to tell Diller how glad we are that he's safe and sound," Jon said. "The world will never know how close it came to losing one of its best unshaven stars." Everyone laughed. "And I just want to say that I've loved working with him and I hope next time we can actually finish the picture."

More laughter, although some of the people sort of coughed and looked at each other.

"What about the surprise?" someone yelled.

"The surprise," Jon said with a smile, rubbing his hands together. "The surprise is a secret. We all have secrets we'd like to bury—and Diller has one, too."

Pete watcher Diller's face closely, but it was blank.

"This isn't the first time Diller's worked on one of my pictures," Jon went on. "As a matter of fact, his first movie was also my first movie."

"Oh, no! Not *Vampire in My Closet*," Diller cried out, hiding his face in mock embarrassment. "That bomb was so terrible the studio never released it. I stank in it."

"You certainly did—but so did I. Back then I don't think people would have looked at me and said I had the makings of a brilliant director," Jon said. Travis paused as though he was waiting for applause. "Ladies and gentlemen and friends, Diller doesn't know this, but I have the only existing print of my first movie, *Vampire in My Closet*, starring Diller Rourke. And it's my pleasure to share this gem right now."

The audience howled and applauded.

"Lights! Camera! Action!" Jon called.

The lights went out and spooky music began as the film rolled.

It was an awful movie. Teenagers at a boarding school were attacked by vampires whose crypts had accidentally been opened by the vibrations of kids disco dancing.

Diller was one of the first to be bitten, so that soon he returned to the screen not as a student but as a vampire. He swept onto the screen in a black cape. His pale face had a fluorescent greenish cast, and the black makeup around his eyes made his cheeks look sunken.

Pete suddenly poked Bob and Jupe so hard that Jupe cried "Ouch!"

"Do you see what I see?" Pete said in a whisper. "Remember that?"

Jupe's smile glowed in the dark. "I remember it perfectly. Diller Rourke was wearing that exact same costume on Halloween—the night he vandalized our headquarters!"

16

The Last Gasp

FOR A MOMENT, A LONG, STARING-IN-SILENCE moment, the Three Investigators didn't move. They couldn't. Their eyes were fixed on the movie screen where Diller Rourke, dressed as a glow-in-the-dark vampire, made his bloodthirsty leaps at people.

"I said we needed him to make a mistake," Bob whispered excitedly. "Way to go, Diller!"

"Now we can prove where Diller was on Halloween," said Pete. "Breaking into our headquarters in that vampire costume. Not being held by kidnappers."

Jupe was excited, too, but more cautious. "We've got a videotape of someone breaking into our headquarters. But the trouble is—we can't really prove that it's Diller," he said. "But if we hurry, maybe we can use the tape to squeeze a confession out of someone."

"I think I'm in love with this plan already," Pete said.

"Good," Jupe said, "because you play a major role in it."

Pete's major role turned out to be driving all the way to Headquarters to grab the videotape and then driving like a maniac back to the party. The trick was to get back *before* the movie was over.

Pete's heart was racing as he quickly put his little Vega through its paces on the way to Rocky Beach. The brakes were pulsating and the accelerator seemed to have a dead spot about halfway down. Why did his car's defects always surface just when he needed it to perform like a champ? That's okay, he told himself. It kept his mind off the ticking clock.

He sprang out of the car as soon as he reached Headquarters and ran in to look through the videotapes. October 29. October 30. October 31! Of course it was exactly where Jupe had filed it. Pete tossed it in the air and caught it for good luck, then hopped in his car and headed back to Bel Air.

The crowd in the spooky gothic house was still watching—and laughing at—*Vampire in My Closet* when Pete returned. He quietly slipped into the projection booth in back of the screening room. Luckily the room was empty. Pete loaded the videotape into a player. Then, with a push of a few buttons, the film projector slowed and stopped. Instantly the video projector took over and the tape of Diller breaking in to headquarters appeared on the screen.

Pete ran to join Jupe and Bob. The audience was laughing louder than ever.

"Great editing, Travis," a young actor called out. "Where was this shot, anyway?"

"What were you doing, Travis? Focusing the camera with your eyes closed?" someone else joked.

At that exact moment Diller kicked in the door to Headquarters on the tape.

"Diller, haven't you ever heard of knocking?" a woman said.

She had said the magic word—"Diller." Now Pete, Jupe, and Bob knew they were almost home.

"Hey—that's not me, man," Diller said, sounding nervous.

All the lights in the screening room snapped on. Jon Travis turned and stared at Diller with cold, killer eyes. "When did you do those scenes?" Jon asked.

Diller's fingers clutched a blue crystal. "I'm telling you, man, that's not me," he said.

"Not you? Of course it's you. It's not Rex the Wonder Horse!" Jon said.

"It's not me," Diller said, weakly this time.

"But Diller," Victoria Jansen said softly, "who else could it be? You know you kept that costume after you finished that movie. Why are you denying it?"

Marble Ackbourne-Smith, who was one of the party guests, stood up and spread his arms wide, as if to silence the already silent crowd. "Sometimes we appear to be the people we are not, even when we are being the people we are," he said.

"Nice try, Marble," Pete called from the back of the room. "But you're still Tommy the Two-Ton Titan or I'll eat my car."

Marble sat down again quickly, and Diller fidgeted in his seat.

"Somebody better start explaining what's going on," Jon Travis said.

Pete, Jupe, and Bob walked quickly, triumphantly, to the front of the room.

"Mr. Travis," Jupe began, "that tape you just saw belongs to us. And it was taped on Halloween, exactly nine days ago—the night Diller Rourke vandalized our headquarters in Rocky Beach."

There was a small gasp from the crowd, then laughter mixed with mumblings of disbelief.

"That's not possible," said Victoria Jansen. "Diller was kidnapped three days before Halloween."

"There never was a kidnapping," Jupe announced. "His disappearance was a hoax."

Suddenly Marty Morningbaum's watch beeped and Marty stood up. "I can't sit here listening to three boys with overstimulated imaginations. They're obviously on drugs. Diller was kidnapped, we all know that. Get rid of them, Travis." He started to push his way up the aisle. But Pete blocked his path.

"Please stay, Mr. Morningbaum," Jupe said. "Your name will be mentioned frequently."

"What's that mean?" asked Jon Travis.

"Ask Diller Rourke," said Pete.

Diller stood up as if he too wanted to leave. But everyone was looking at him—and he had to perform. He looked at Marty, then at Jupe, Pete, and Bob. Pete thought he looked for all the world like a cornered animal.

Finally Diller sat back down, perching on the top of his movie theater chair.

"Yeah, okay, I was never kidnapped, okay? It was just a joke."

"A joke? You call sabotaging my film a joke!" Jon shouted angrily. "How could you do that to me?"

Marty Morningbaum sat down disgustedly. "I know. It probably would have been easier just to kill you, Jon. That way we'd be sure you'd never make another movie again."

"Grow up and face the facts, man. *Suffocation II* was going to be a total bomb," Diller said. "The best parts of that movie were awful. I guess you just couldn't handle the big leagues, Jon."

"Says who?" shouted Travis.

"I do, for one," Marty Morningbaum said.

Diller laughed ironically and looked into his blue crystal. "I'll tell you what went down, so you can all get a laugh," he said to the crowd. "A couple weeks ago Marty and I were looking at some dailies. And he was just getting sicker and sicker. Finally he told me he had lost a bundle on the movie already, and if he finished it he'd lose twenty million more. Hey—it was going to be *Vampire in My Closet* all over again. I knew if this movie got released, my career would go down the tubes faster than bacon grease. So when Marty laid out a plan to me, I said go for it. No hard feelings, Travis."

"No hard feelings," Jon agreed. "As long as you and Marty go to jail."

"Jail?" Diller walked to the front and stood by the screen. "Hey, no way. Maybe we were playing a little dirty, okay? But that's just because it was this great double part. I got to be the victim *and* the kidnapper. So I really started getting into the kidnapper's head.

You know, like tearing my house apart. It looked like a hurricane, didn't it?"

"The glass," Pete interrupted, suddenly feeling like he couldn't breathe again. "What was all the broken glass?"

"An inspiration," Diller said. "See, like I needed my crystals with me. But I keep them in a glass display case at home. I knew if the police came, they would wonder what was in the case and why it was gone. It would be suspicious, man, if the kidnappers let me take the crystals along."

"So to make the whole scene look even more violent you smashed the display case," Jupe said. "Hence, broken glass covering the floors."

"Yeah," Diller said. "This kidnapper was one bad dude. Like, when I was on the playground to pick up the ransom money, for a second I just went wild. You guys were chasing me and I smacked someone with the suitcase as hard as I could. It was unbelievable how this guy took over."

"Yeah, unbelievable," Pete said, remembering how it felt to have the air knocked out of him.

"On Halloween night we had only been on the case a few hours," Jupe said. "Why did you tear up our headquarters?"

"Marty told me about you guys," Diller said, "and the kidnapper inside me went nuts. I figured he'd want to scare you off the trail fast."

"I *told* you not to do it," Marty blurted out. "I *told* you it was risky. But no. You always have to overact."

"Hey, look. What's the crime?" Diller said. "So one movie didn't get made. No big thing—America won't miss it. And as for taking a week off, I saved my career and got a million bucks."

"You got to keep the ransom money?" Pete asked.

"Yeah," said Diller. "It's half the money the insurance company paid Marty. I guess I'll have to give it back now, huh?"

Pete nodded. "Yeah, but you got burned, slick," he said. "Marty's check from the insurance company read twenty million dollars."

Diller's head jerked toward Marty.

"Ha!" said Jon Travis. "That's what you get for believing a producer. They'll always try to underpay you. All actors are children."

"And all directors are egomaniacs," Diller said bitterly.

The room was quiet until someone suddenly got up to leave.

"Victoria, where are you going?" Diller called out.

Victoria Jansen was almost out the door, but she turned back to Diller. "I don't want to stay for the end of the story. I know how it turns out," she said sadly. "The police come and take away the criminals. It wasn't your best role, Diller. I wish you had stuck to playing heroes."

After she left, the party broke up quickly. Marty Morningbaum kept promising a complete explanation but no one stayed to listen to it.

"The police will listen, Mr. Morningbaum," Jupiter

said, looking at his watch. "I called them a few minutes ago."

It took most of the night to get all of the stories down on paper at the precinct. When the Three Investigators left, the sun was coming up. It was time to go back to Rocky Beach and their normal lives. They went to school a few hours later. Then Pete and Bob worked after school. And Jupe filed the paperwork on their case and tinkered with a new electronics project.

Usually the trio talked a lot about the most recently solved case. But not this time. They had solved it and they had won—but it was the one that almost got away. It felt unfinished somehow.

Then, several days later, Pete arrived at Headquarters with a letter from Marty Morningbaum. He spread the note on the desk so Bob and Jupe could read it too.

Dear Pete,
—I must confess—something I have been doing frequently these days—that I completely underestimated you and your two companions. But you'll be happy to know that through my attorneys I have been able to settle this matter with the insurance company and square matters for Diller as well. As for my future, thanks to you I won't work in Hollywood again—not for the next three of four months, anyway. Fortunately for me, this industry has a very short memory. By next spring all of this will have blown over and will be forgotten. So that's

what I'm writing to you about. When I make my
return, I want to film a mystery, a mystery about a
fake kidnapping. Let's have lunch—no more doped
milk shakes, I promise!—and discuss the movie
rights to your story about how you and your friends
solved the crime. Working title for the project: *The
Making of a Great Suffocation*.

Bob was the first to speak after they read the letter.
"I don't believe the guy. He came this close to getting
his butt thrown in jail and he wants to turn it into a
moneymaking opportunity! Should we flip to see who
gets to tear that letter up?"

Without waiting, Pete ripped the letter to shreds
and threw it into the wastebasket. "There!" he said
with satisfaction. "*Now* this case feels complete!"

Pete was going to say something more, but suddenly
he couldn't. That suffocating feeling was starting
again. "I can't breathe," he said with a gasp. "Every
time I think about this case or even hear the word
'suffocation,' I can't breathe."

"Try to relax, Pete," said Jupe. "I've been meaning
to tell you about that."

"What is it, Jupe?" Pete asked. "Hypnotic suggestion? The crystals? Is it a jinx or something Marble
did? What's doing this to me?"

Jupe calmly reached into his desk and pulled out a
newspaper clipping. He handed it to Pete. "It's another
mystery I've solved. I think this will explain it," Jupe
said.

Pete read the newspaper headline and his mouth

dropped open. It said: *Pollen Count Up 500% In Longest Ragweed Season Ever*.

"It's not *The Suffocation*, and it's not a jinx," Jupe said. "It's just hay fever, Pete."

"Aaachoo!" gasped Pete.